No Happy Ending

Paco Ignacio Taibo II

translated by William I. Neuman

Poisoned Pen Press

Copyright © 1981 byPaco Ignacio Taibo II

First Trade Paperback Edition 2003

10 9 8 7 6 5 4 3 2 1

Library of Congress Catalog Card Number: 2002114512

ISBN: 1-59058-038-9   Trade Paperback

Poisoned Pen Press
6962 E. First Ave. Ste 103
Scottsdale, AZ 85251
www.poisonedpenpress.com
info@poisonedpenpress.com

Printed in the United States of America

No Happy Ending

Also by the author
An Easy Thing
Some Clouds

For Paloma (La Pecas), always

...send me books with happy endings,
where the airplane lands without mishap,
the surgeon leaves the operating room with a smile
    on his face,
the blind boy's eyes are opened,
the young man is saved from the firing squad,
people are reunited,
where there are parties and weddings.
                                —*Nazim Hikmet*

Deaf country, burned city,
the bonfire calls us,
in these times,
    there will be no happy ending.
                                —*PIT II*

Chapter I

New times overtake me. Overtake my yearnings.

—Piero

There's a dead Roman in the bathroom."

"When he's done pissing tell him to drop by and say hello," said Héctor Belascoarán Shayne.

A late, lazy, hot afternoon lingered outside the window.

"This isn't a joke," said the upholsterer Carlos Vargas from the doorway.

Héctor stared out at the clouds moving slowly over his piece of city. "Does he have a spear? Any Roman worth his salt's got to have a spear."

"I said he's dead!"

Héctor got up from the leather swivel chair where he'd whiled away what was left of the afternoon, and looked carefully at his officemate.

The upholsterer leaned against the doorjamb, his face pale, distractedly swinging a small hammer in one hand.

With a limp that was due partly to an old wound and partly because he'd left one shoe behind him under the desk, Héctor walked toward the door. He raised his left hand to his head and ran it roughly through his hair, as if to physically shake off his drowsiness.

"What about a helmet? Has he got a helmet?" Héctor tried one last joke, but the upholsterer's expression didn't change.

Was there really a dead Roman in the bathroom?

Carlos led the way down the ruined hall, the afternoon light filtering through the doorway onto the peeling walls painted a malignant green.

"Yes, he's got a helmet," said Carlos as he pushed open the bathroom door.

A Roman foot soldier sat on the toilet, staring at the tile floor, his throat slashed.

Blood oozed slowly down the brass breastplate, over the short, pleated skirt, the hairy legs, and into one sandal. A helmet with a faded plume rested on his head. A long wooden spear leaned against the wall.

"They've gone too far this time," Héctor muttered, cautiously lifting the Roman's chin. A four-inch gash cut across his throat.

"Who?"

"The sons of bitches who killed this guy."

The dead man looked at Héctor through bugged-out eyes. He was about fifty years old, with a stubbly growth of beard above a thick double chin. Héctor couldn't keep a shiver from running up his spine despite the absurdity of the situation.

He let go of the chin and the head sagged back toward the man's chest, partly covering the gash across his throat. There was blood on Héctor's hand. He wiped it off on the Roman's skirt.

"So what do we do now?"

"We search him," said Belascoarán, inserting his hand behind the metal breastplate etched with dragons and swords and into the pocket of a shirt cut off at the sleeves to give the Roman an authentic, period look.

"Car keys, a hundred pesos, an advertisement for a tailor's shop, an electric bill…" he recited as he brought the items out and stashed each one in his pants pocket.

"There's something in his sock," said Carlos, pointing.

Héctor pulled a plastic-coated ID card from one of the dead man's incongruous socks and shoved it in his pocket without looking at it.

"Let's go, neighbor."

"Where to?"

"Anywhere but here. I don't like this. You can't just let people go around killing Romans in your bathroom."

The upholsterer, hammer in hand, turned back toward the office. Héctor got there before him.

The afternoon was starting to fade. He found his shoe under the wingback chair, collected his jacket from the coatrack, took his .45 automatic from his desk drawer, and slid it into his shoulder holster. They locked the office door behind them.

At that moment the elevator motor kicked into action.

"Quick! The stairs!"

"What if it's Gilberto?" asked the detective.

The two men eyed the metal grating. A song rose up from the elevator shaft, over the noise from the motor and the stillness of their held-in breath: a *ranchera*, sung loudly and off-key.

"It's Gilberto," said Héctor. Carlos nodded.

"What's up?" asked the plumber—the third member of that strange community that occupied the fourth-floor office of the building on the corner of Bucareli and Artículo 123—as the elevator door slid open.

"Let's go," said Héctor, pushing Gilberto back into the elevator, with Carlos right behind him.

"What's the big hurry? A guy comes into work feeling like getting something done for a change, and they won't even let him into his own office," Gilberto protested unsuccessfully.

"There's a dead Roman in the bathroom," said Carlos.

"Roman? Like a Roman orgy kind of Roman?" Gilberto Gómez Letras asked with sudden interest.

"He's got his fucking throat cut from here to here," said Carlos, with an appropriately emphatic gesture.

"Yeah, right. What're you guys trying to pull? Let's see… what'd you do, go and hire a secretary behind my back and you've been up there balling her all afternoon…"

Héctor leaned silently in one corner of the elevator. Who would want to get him mixed up in a murder like this? And what for? What was the idea of killing a guy dressed up like a Roman soldier?

"…what's her name, Amber Eden, Graciela Putricia?"

The elevator door opened and the three men went out, Gilberto still trying to convince his friends to let him go up and meet the new secretary.

Dodging traffic, they crossed the street and went into a Chinese restaurant. Héctor chose a booth where he could watch the door to their building. It was starting to get dark.

"Two *cafés con leche*, donuts, and a hot chocolate," said Héctor to the restaurant's owner. "Now let me think for a minute."

"It's no joke, Gilberto, there really is a dead Roman up there."

"Yeah, right. So what's her name?"

"Forget it, Gilberto. You don't have what it takes. All you'll ever have is those hookers you like so much out in Nezahualcóyotl. You want a secretary, you got to show some class."

The traffic got heavier. A pair of shoeshine boys played soccer between the cars with a ball of wadded-up paper.

"There goes El Gallo. Go get him and bring him over here," said Héctor. The upholsterer, who was sitting closest to the door, jumped up and ran out into the street. A car braked noisily.

A moment later, the sewer engineer Javier Villareal, alias El Gallo, sat in the booth with his three officemates.

"What's going on around here?"

"Will you believe me if I tell you there's a dead Roman in our bathroom?" asked Héctor.

"What can I say? In the two years since I've been sharing an office with you, I've seen two shootouts, a case of poisoned soft drinks, and a kindergarten party. One time Gilberto rented it out as a practice space for a salsa band, and another time some old geezer tried to stab me with a knife. What's a dead Roman to me?"

"You guys aren't fooling, are you?" asked Gilberto.

"Hot chocolate and donuts," ordered El Gallo.

Early the next morning a motorcycle messenger delivered a manila envelope to Héctor Belascoarán Shayne's apartment, pocketed his tip, and drove away. Héctor stood watching after him in the open doorway, bleary-eyed, the envelope in his hand.

After gulping down two glasses of grapefruit juice mixed from a greenish powder, he sat down at the kitchen table and tore open the envelope: there was a half sheet of paper with the typewritten message, "Don't get involved," an airplane ticket to New York made out in his name, and a Polaroid snapshot of a man whose throat had been hacked open with a knife.

Death. All over again.

He spent the next ten minutes looking for his cigarettes. He finally found them under his pillow on his bed, then he shut the door to his apartment, which he'd left open, and went back to the kitchen table to stare at the photograph.

It was too early in the morning. This time of day always threw him off balance, the way it was so empty, sluggish, unreal somehow. It made it so that he didn't know who he was, couldn't recognize himself.

Even with his graying crew cut the dead man in the picture was still a little younger than the Roman had been. He had a square face and a hard jaw. That's all Héctor could tell, with the head thrown backward like that. The man sat on a chair with his hands tied behind him to the chair back, with something that didn't look like rope. Wire maybe.

A cop, thought Héctor, without knowing why. Maybe because of the crew cut, or the cheap gray suit that gave him the vague look of the secret police. Or a doorman in a four-star hotel. Or a loan shark.

What the hell did all this have to do with him? He wasn't working on anything, he'd spent the last two months in a kind of quasi-Buddhist contemplation of the downtown streets, going on endless, meandering walks, poking around tenement buildings, hunting for bargains in second-hand bookstores, watching the clouds or the traffic from his office window. Two months waiting for something that was worth getting excited about. And now this: two dead men and a plane ticket to New York to keep him from sticking his nose in where somebody thought it didn't belong. But if they didn't want him to get involved, then why the hell had they gone and dumped a dead Roman in his bathroom, and then sent him the photograph of this other guy?

The hot water heater was broken, but he went and took a shower anyway. He stood under the cold spray, and came to a decision that was out of character for him: he would wait one more day, and then decide whether to step aside, or to dig deeper into the story. Two minutes later he changed his mind.

"New York my ass!" he said, shivering with cold.

✢ ✣ ✢

He walked cautiously down the hall and opened the door to the bathroom only to discover the obvious (who knows why, who knows how, but obvious enough in the end): the dead Roman had disappeared. All that was left was a brownish bloodstain on the floor, and a certain vague smell that Héctor Belascoarán Shayne, independent detective, would forever after associate with the smell left behind by death.

He shut the door again and turned to look at his three officemates watching curiously from the far end of the hall.

"He's not there. Must have gone for a walk," Belascoarán said laconically.

"I never even got to see him," complained Gilberto.

"You didn't miss much. What good's a Roman with socks?" observed the upholsterer.

Héctor left them in the hall and went into the office.

The night before, he'd kept watch from the Chinese restaurant across the street until after midnight, when fatigue had gotten the better of him and he'd gone home. All the same, it made him feel good; at least his intuition was still working.

He took his coat from the rack and was about to head out again when the telephone rang. El Gallo Villareal looked up from his drawing table, where he sat doodling a naked woman perched on a tall stool.

"Aren't you here kind of early, Gallo?"

"I wanted to see the Roman."

"Sorry to disappoint you," said Héctor, picking up the phone.

On the other end, his sister, Elisa, asked him over for lunch. He said yes without thinking twice, then went down to the street.

He felt the cool air on his face as he left the building, and a muscle tensed near the scar that trailed away from his bad eye. It was always with him, unseeing, useless, reminding him how close a man could come, how easy it was, how quickly everything could go to hell, how tremendously screwed up this country was. Not to mention his job.

Methodically, he set about finding a witness to the dead Roman's disappearance. He came up empty-handed at the record store, the Chinese restaurant across the street, and with Doña Concha, the woman who cleaned their building. But he hit gold with Salustio, the one-eyed man who ran the newspaper kiosk on the corner.

At six A.M. two men had come out of the building carrying a box, "like for a small refrigerator," and loaded it into a moving van. At the same time the picture of the second victim had been delivered to the detective's apartment. But Salustio couldn't give him a description of the men or their vehicle. He said he was sorry.

"With just one eye I don't see too good at six in the morning, and with the hangover I had this morning, you're lucky I saw as much as I did."

Héctor slipped off into the passing human torrent, hoping that the rhythm of his walking would help to put his thoughts in order. He lit a cigarette and set off at a brisk pace through the downtown streets.

What was going on? If they didn't want him to get involved, what were they doing sending him dead bodies? And what did the Roman have to do with it?

Ixtapalapa? The passion play? No, this was December, not Holy Week. No connection there.

He walked across the Alameda park, watching two small children tag along after a balloonman. At Avenida Hidalgo he joined a crowd gathered around a police van that had caught fire from a short circuit under the hood.

Two policemen were trying to put out the fire while the crowd watched. No one volunteered to lend a hand. Mexicans love a spectacle as much as they hate the law, he thought, as the fire flared up with a beautiful explosion of flame and fireworks. The hundred or so onlookers broke into applause, then started to retreat before the hateful stare of one of the policemen, who held a Mauser in his hands.

"Helluva show," said a lottery ticket seller.

Héctor nodded.

"Too bad it didn't blow up and take those two sons of bitches with it," said a high school student loaded down with books, as he hurried past Héctor to catch his bus.

"Too bad," said the woman who sold ears of boiled corn from a pushcart, whom the two cops had been shaking down when their van caught fire.

"Too bad," repeated Héctor. He lit another cigarette and went off to keep his lunch date.

"You know him better than I do. You tell me. Should I be worried, or am I just imagining things?"

"What the hell do I know? I can't figure him out either. Him and his friends, they talk in a language I can't understand. They're dealing with bigger things than anything I could ever lay claim to. I've got nothing—"

"Okay, Héctor, that's enough. The complaints window is closed for the afternoon," said Elisa, as she set the table with plates, glasses, salt and pepper shakers, paper napkins, and a tureen of hearty beef stew. Héctor laughed, really laughed, for the first time in a couple of days. He'd been working so hard at keeping his emotions under control that his face had become frozen into a sort of crooked sneer.

"So he's been drinking. What else is going on?"

"Isn't that enough? What's he need to drink so much for?"

"What are you getting at, Elisa? Do you think he's in some kind of trouble? What is it?"

"I think he's gotten himself involved in something really heavy this time. I don't know anything for sure, it's just a feeling. The two times I saw him this week he seemed depressed, down, you know. Once he was drunk, and the other time I went by his apartment and he was sleeping. The whole place smelled like rum."

"Are you sure?"

"I didn't dare say anything. I mean, it's not my business, really…I feel like an idiot, but I can't even talk to my own kid brother."

"The same thing happens to me when I try and talk to you, silly."

Elisa gave Héctor a hug. Her freckles shone in the sunlight angling through the window into the small apartment.

"I asked him to come and have lunch with us. He said he was busy but he'd try and get here in time for coffee."

"Listen, if *you* can't talk to him, then forget it, because I'm a hundred times worse than you are. I'm sure that…"

The doorbell rang as they were drinking coffee, remembering afternoons spent in the old house in Coyoacán, and their father, old man Belascoarán, with his leftist-inspired stories of life in the Wild West, Wild Bill Hickock, Billy the Kid.

"*Jefe!*" howled a blond, freckled shadow as it threw itself into the arms of a disconcerted, shy, but happy Héctor Belascoarán Shayne.

After Marina came their brother, Carlos Brian. Three or four years younger than Héctor, he had his mother's Irish genes, a thick mop of red hair, and extraordinarily blue eyes. Extraordinarily blue and extraordinarily tired, thought Héctor, taking a second, closer look at his brother, while he tried to disentangle himself from Marina.

"Well if it isn't my big brother," said Carlos, patting him softly on the cheek.

"How long has it been, *jefe?*"

"A couple of years, Marina."

The three of them went into the dining room, which doubled occasionally as a guest bedroom. Elisa had gone into the kitchen to make more coffee.

"What are you up to these days, brother?" asked Carlos.

"The worst part of it is I don't even know myself."

Héctor hesitated, caught between the urge to tell them about the dead Roman in the office bathroom and the dead man in the photograph—and the temptation to retreat into his habitual reticence.

"What about you guys?" he asked, opting to take himself out of the ring.

"We're going to have a baby," said Marina, placing her hand on a stomach just beginning to grow big.

"Seriously?" asked Elisa, returning with a steaming pot of coffee.

"Seriously," said Carlos.

Héctor took out his pack of Delicado filters and lit one.

I'm going to be an uncle, he thought. He didn't feel like getting involved in his brother's life, he didn't need any more problems. Suddenly he realized that he was tired too. Tired of what? he asked himself.

"I'm tired too," he announced, as though someone there could tell him why.

"You and who else?" asked Carlos.

"You, apparently," Elisa cut in.

"Wait a minute. If this is what you guys have in mind, then I'm out of here. If we're going to play family Ping-Pong, I'm going to take my paddle and go."

"Tell it to him straight, Elisa," said Héctor, picking up his coffee cup and cradling it in his hands, avoiding his brother's eyes.

"Me? I'm the subject of the family reunion?" asked Carlos with a laugh. "I thought it was you," he said, pointing at Héctor.

Marina sat down on the rug in a corner of the room.

"I suppose it could just as easily be me," said Elisa, with a warm smile in Marina's direction.

"What's wrong?" Marina asked.

"I guess we're kind of a weird family," said Héctor.

"What you are is a bunch of cowards," said Marina.

They drank their coffee in silence. Out in the street, a child went by pulling a wagon, and the screech of the wheels came to them through the window.

"Something's going on, though, isn't it, Carlos?" asked Elisa. "Besides the baby, I mean."

"Uh-huh."

"Tell them already, dammit. You're acting like you don't trust them," said Marina, looking Carlos in the eye.

"Some other time. I'm not having a very good day today." He stood up. "Thanks for the coffee, Elisa. You coming?" he asked Marina on his way out the door.

Marina got up, kissed Elisa, and held Héctor's hand for a moment.

"See you later, *jefe*. Let me know if you ever need a secretary again. I've got lots of free time on my hands."

She went out, leaving the door open behind her. Héctor looked out into the empty hallway in silence, thinking about how he loved them both.

"So much for our family meeting," said Elisa. "More coffee?"

"No thanks, I've got to get moving. I'm going to be an uncle. And you're going to be an aunt. Can you believe it?"

❖ ❖ ❖

Maybe because he understood that loneliness doesn't kill, but that it's lonely people who go off and die on their own, Héctor had learned to engage himself in an intense internal monologue while he moved through the city, glomming distractedly on to little fragments of the urban landscape as he went, Christmas decorations, faces, blotches of color, voices, noises, impressions.

Without knowing how he'd got there, he found himself back in the center of town. It was rush hour, all the shops were full, car horns sounded amidst lights and more lights. He felt insulated by the tumult, anonymous in the bustling crowd, and he concentrated his energy inward, inside his head. At Donceles he came to a café where an old man stood playing "Veracruz" on the clarinet. He drank a soda pop and listened to the wistful, romantic melody, observing the unhappy relationship between the musician and his audience. When the old man was done, the detective followed him into a bar, where he played the same song again, only to be met by the same impassive expression on the faces of his accidental listeners. As though the old man wasn't even there, had never been there. He followed him into an oyster bar twenty paces down the street toward San Juan de Letran. And then to a juice bar after that.

For the fourth time, the blind old man passed the hat in front of Héctor, and for the fourth time, Héctor dropped a couple of peso coins inside, the last of his change.

"Excuse me, don't you know how to play anything except 'Veracruz'?"

"Sure I do. But I had a girlfriend from there once, and I've been thinking about her a lot lately," said the old man.

Héctor quit following him. All he had left was a five-hundred-peso bill, and he didn't want to keep on listening if he wasn't going to give something in return. The old man raised his clarinet to his lips, blowing the first few notes of "Veracruz," the song and the instrument both relics of a better time, better memories. No one in the juice bar paid him any attention, despite the fact that there was a long line of people waiting to buy haw-apple juice, the advertised special of the day.

"You learn something new every day," Héctor told himself. He wasn't even sure he knew what a haw-apple was, let alone that you could make juice out of it. He headed over to Artículo 123 and his office.

As he climbed the stairs, he could feel the fatigue come over him from so many hours of brisk walking on pavement.

"All's quiet, neighbor," said El Gallo Villareal, who sat hunched over his blueprints.

"They didn't bring any new corpses dressed up like Nezahualcóyotl?"

"They must have the day off."

Héctor collapsed into the big armchair. Its springs creaked with a delicious intimacy under his weight. I love this fucking chair, Héctor thought.

What the hell is going on?

Héctor sunk even deeper into the old leather. The air was full of smoke from El Gallo's cigar. Outside, the sweet night. Here, the warm, familiar office, a couple of dead men hovering around out there somewhere. Too peaceful by far. Héctor didn't want to think about any of it. His thoughts returned to the old blind man, the way he swayed back and forth on the tips of his toes, the out-of-tune, metallic sound of the clarinet in the midst of the traffic noise, the sweet, catchy melody.

"Tell me something. You're a scientist…"

"I'm only a scientist when it comes to building sewers, neighbor. For the rest of it, I've just got a good eye, that's all."

"Me, I'm the opposite…I decided to become a detective because I didn't like the color my wife picked for the new carpet. I got my license by mail for three hundred pesos, and I've never read a single British mystery novel. I don't know a fingerprint from a finger sandwich. I can only shoot something if it doesn't move very much. All that and I'm only thirty-three years old."

"Well, let's just hope you make it."

"Make what?"

"To thirty-four."

There was a long pause. Héctor lit a cigarette.

"I don't understand a thing. Not one damn thing," he said, throwing the match onto the floor and giving up on his officemate's scientific opinion.

He was becoming quite a talker. He preferred his old style, the taciturn and enigmatic Belascoarán Shayne. The other face of the clueless, uneasy, perennially surprised Belascoarán Shayne. The public face. Because, when all is said and done, a man is a hunter after images. After his own image. Sometimes he's successful in the hunt and he comes up with something consistent, warm, something close to reality. Other times he spends all night pursuing an illusion, clinging to shadows. And sometimes the shadow turns around and comes after him, and everything goes to hell. His only chance for survival was to accept the chaos and quietly become one with it. Take yourself lightly, but take the city seriously, the city, that inscrutable porcupine bristling with quills and soft wrinkles. Shit, he was in love with Mexico City. Another impossible love on his list. A city to love, to love with abandon. Passionately, wildly.

Héctor's mind fed off all this and more (the cold air, the *ranchera* music drifting up from the record store, the roofs of buses passing before his eyes without really registering) as he watched the street from the roof of his office building, where he'd gone to smoke a cigarette, to pursue the night, watching from above, keeping his distance.

The best thing was to wait. The killers would show their faces sooner or later. He tossed his cigarette over the edge and watched the tiny spark's descent with pleasure, a dot of light slowly dropping the seven floors to the street.

✣ ✣ ✣

"His name is Rataplan," said the woman with the ponytail.

Héctor, who'd just come from the kitchen with a knife in one hand and a pair of eggs in the other, didn't know quite how to react to the small rabbit that was unceremoniously thrust between his arms.

Smiling and implacable, humming the theme from *Casablanca*, the woman with the ponytail held out the black rabbit.

"Boy or girl?" asked the detective, blocking the door with his body.

"It's a boy, stupid. Obviously. I wouldn't bring you a girl bunny."

"I guess you can come in then."

Héctor turned his back on her and retreated into the kitchen.

"Put on the record that's on the record player. Start it on the second song."

"What is it?"

"Gerry Mulligan."

The oil smoked in the pan, the onion was starting to burn. He dumped some of the oil into the sink, then broke the eggs into the pan. So much for my omelette, he thought.

Failure alienates, fear destroys one's willingness to try new things and attracts more fear, life runs away. There was a lot to think about, but Héctor wasn't in the mood for licking at his wounds, so he just stood there instead, mumbling incoherently to himself, watching the eggs cook. In the living room, the woman with the ponytail finally figured out how to operate the dilapidated record player and Mulligan's sax filled the air.

"Do you want me to go?"

"What?"

"Do you want me to go away?"

Héctor hesitated. "Yes."

"I'm leaving you the rabbit," she said, and disappeared.

Héctor listened to the door close, then hurried into the hallway to bring her back, to shout without shouting for her to not go away, fighting against the urge to take her by the arm and stop her. When he got back to the kitchen his omelette was burned beyond all salvation.

"You know what?" Héctor asked out loud.

The rabbit looked at him for a moment, then went back to nibbling on a stray boot lying in the middle of the floor.

"I'm never going to fall in love with a woman again."

The rabbit raised its eyes at this macabre declaration, and tilted its ears forward.

"I'm never going to be able to have a stable relationship with anyone again."

The rabbit directed an appropriately harsh stare in the detective's direction.

"And the worst of it is that I knew it all along."

The rabbit turned his back on Héctor and pissed on the rug.

Héctor smiled, laughed, and started to cry.

He had two dead men, one plastic ID card, an electric bill, a photograph, a possible lead in the messenger service that had brought him the photo, and a one-way ticket to New York. That was all. It wasn't much, but it was better than standing around crying in a corner of the room while he waited for the smoke from the burned omelette to clear. If he got to work right now he'd gain a day, instead of waiting passively for who knows what to happen.

He turned the record player up all the way and tried to think. Mulligan's music was like a soft, fuzzy caress. Like the rabbit, if it could play the saxophone.

The ID card bore the name *Leobardo Martínez Reta*, giving the aforementioned the right to the rather dubious discounts offered to state employees in the government-run stores of the social security system. Why carry it around in his sock? The card didn't give any information about the man's background or employment. He couldn't even be sure that this Leobardo Martínez was actually the dead Roman. Who knows? Maybe he'd picked it up off the floor and stuck it in his sock. The electric bill came from a carpenter's shop on Bolívar Street.

One question bothered him more than the rest. If they'd gone to all the trouble of carting the body away again, why hadn't they thought to remove the ID card and the electric bill in the first place, after they killed him? The messenger service was bound to be a waste of time; he gave up on the hope of finding anything there. The plane ticket was for the next day, at twelve noon.

A good time to fly to New York. A good time not to fly to New York. Mulligan had the air all to himself; the rabbit had taken possession of the rug. What did rabbits eat? What did saxophonists eat? What did dead Romans eat? What could a detective eat, after burning his omelette all to hell?

Chapter II

The blood never stops until it reaches the river.
—*Alberto Hidalgo*

This what you're looking for?"

Héctor nodded. The bodies of the two dead men lay on the metal table, their throats cut.

"Have they been identified? Does anybody know anything about them?"

"Around here, the less you know the better. All we can do is try and make sure the stiffs don't end up as taco meat," the attendant said, laughing.

Héctor took out a hundred-peso bill and handed it to the man, who stashed it in his uniform pocket.

"They found 'em together, stripped naked just like you see 'em here. Out by El Molinito, on the Toluca highway. The cop who does the paperwork around here came down to have a look at 'em, and then one of the big cheeses showed up, a group commander, some guy I'd never seen around here before. I guess there must be something about it that's got their attention…Take a look at the way the two of 'em had their throats cut. It's almost the same. And one of 'em has marks on his wrists like they had him tied up…"

Héctor took a closer look at the two naked, bluish cadavers. Both men were about fifty years old, muscular but past their prime, dark complexion, dark hair going gray. There was something sad about them, as though they didn't like being dead. Héctor knew them both. One he knew from a photograph. The other one he recognized even without his red-plumed Roman helmet.

"Who did you say was the commander in charge of the investigation?"

"The group commander...I think they called him Major Silva. A major idiot, if you ask me. He comes down, takes one quick look and says, Keep 'em on ice for me. He didn't even take a good look at 'em, didn't even examine 'em. Not like me."

Héctor walked out of the morgue. He started to whistle a tune, then paused to think of something appropriate. Something to take away the sickly smell and the sight of the twin slashed throats. A bossa nova, perhaps, or a samba...He thought it over, decided on "Corcovado," and went on his way.

❖ ❖ ❖

The tenement house on Bolívar Street was surrounded by cantinas, a tiny rat's nest of a watch shop, and a small wooden hanger factory—you could watch them sanding the hangers through the open shopfront. Across the street, in front of an ironwork shop where they made window gratings, a worker stood playing with a yo-yo and airing his stomach, away from the heat of the furnace. Héctor Belascoarán Shayne, independent detective, paused to check the lay of the land.

He wasn't feeling particularly intelligent, particularly aggressive or bold. He needed to take a moment to sharpen his senses, to let the atmosphere of the place sink in, and to break through the sense of apathy that had been dogging him all day long.

He pushed off from the wall and approached the tenement, stepping inside over a pair of children playing marbles in the open doorway. He climbed up a dirty, creaking wooden stairway two floors to the roof, where a pair of women were washing clothes.

"Number B? The carpenter's?"

One of the women pointed to a large door farther along the roof.

He followed the whine of a band saw to the shop, where two men, naked from the waist up, worked hurriedly in a storm of sawdust.

"Sorry, mister, we're closing up," one of them said when Héctor reached the open doorway.

"The boss kicked off and we've got to go to the wake," said the other one, his face lit up by a broad grin under a backward baseball cap.

"Where's the wake? In the old man's house?"

"No, in La Numantina. Just for friends, that means me and him," the man said, pointing a thumb at his partner.

"I knew the old man. Can I come along?"

"In that cantina, whoever pays, plays, *jefe.*"

No matter how much he insisted, they wouldn't let Héctor switch from cheap Madero brandy to grapefruit soda, so somewhere around the third glass he suddenly found himself embarked on an uncertain path through the intricate labyrinth of his own self-reflection.

If life is that period of time that runs from the instant the doctor picks you up by your feet and waits for you to start crying, until the moment when your old friends raise a glass in memory of your passing, then the measure of a man's life comes down to how many old and good friends he's been able to make and hold on to over the years. It was a complicated equation, because it meant not only that your friends should be truly faithful, but that they should remain alive, in the best sense of the word. And for a man to have truly noble friends it was necessary for him to live on noble terms both with them and with his country. The carpenter who had owned the little rooftop shop on Bolívar Street had evidently failed this ultimate test, if he was to be judged by the pair of hardened alcoholics who today toasted his demise. But what about Héctor? How many lunatics would take the death of Héctor Belascoarán Shayne as an occasion for reunion, remembrance, and love? He asked for another Madero, knocking it back in a single shot before the hostile gaze of the bartender, who, no matter how hard Héctor tried to disguise it, saw him for the unrepentant teetotaler that he normally was. Then he started to count off on his fingers. There were his three officemates, Gilberto the plumber, Carlos Vargas the upholsterer, and the sewer engineer El Gallo Villareal. Over the last three years they'd built an intimate bond out of their diverse professions and attitudes toward life; but theirs was more than a simple friendship, it had to do with a way they had of maintaining a certain perspective toward the country as a whole, of isolating themselves from all the screwed-up shit it threw at them every day. Then there was his deejay friend, El Cuervo Valdivia; and Carlos and Elisa, his brother and sister, with whom he had formed a sort of familial redoubt of Mafia-like solidarity. There was Father Rosales, the priest from Culhuacán, with whom he'd gotten involved in that mess at the Basílica; and the singer Benigno Padilla, Benny the King, whose life he'd saved; and the Reyna brothers, union activists he'd worked with; Mendiola, the reporter, who'd reemerged from the forgotten past of his school days, just like El Cuervo had; and Maldonado too, a lawyer and heroin addict, permanently flirting with the abyss, with whom Héctor was united by a common faith in the constant, inevitable proximity of death. That was it. All of them were either new friends he'd met during the last three years of detective work, or old friends he'd recovered in that same time. He'd salvaged nothing else from the remote past. And what about all the women he'd loved, and who'd loved him, Belascoarán wondered. Could he also add them to the list?

No one but the two carpenters had shown up for the old man's wake. The cantina was strangely quiet. A university student sat at a corner table downing glass after glass of tequila, convinced that was the only appropriate activity for a man whose girlfriend had just left him. An elderly bureaucrat played solitaire at another table. The only other people in the cantina, besides the bartender, were the two carpenters and Héctor, downing one Maderito after another.

"Didn't Don Leobardo have any other friends?" asked Héctor.

"Stupid old fart. Sorry, was he a friend of yours?"

"No, I just knew him in passing."

"He was from Durango, and he'd done just about everything there was to do, been just about everywhere. And he still didn't have any friends. That's how much of an asshole he was."

"He didn't have any friends at all?"

"Well, sure, he used to hang out with those two wackos he worked for Zorak with. What were their names?" the younger one asked his partner.

The older carpenter burped. "Those were his glory days. When Zorak used to let him carry his fucking suitcase."

"What did he do for Zorak?" asked Héctor, intrigued.

"He used to blow on his balls to cool them off when he came through the ring of fire," the man answered mysteriously.

"He filed down the locks for him."

"He sealed up the barrel when they dumped him into Lake Chapultepec."

"I'll bet he was even the one who hooked up the cable on the helicopter."

They kicked the ball back and forth, while Héctor tried to imagine who Zorak was, and what his connection had been to the dead man.

"He was definitely the one who tied the cable," said the younger of the two, and he let out a rough laugh.

"Where can I find Zorak?" asked the detective shyly.

"He's with Don Leobardo," said the younger one.

"He's dead?"

"He fell from a helicopter six years ago. In the middle of one of his stupid shows."

"He wanted to be an angel," said the younger one, who was pretty drunk by now.

"He got his wish," said the other one.

"What did Don Leobardo have to do with it?"

"He was one of Zorak's flunkies...You know, bring me my cape, Don Leobar, bring me my sharp knives so I can stick them up my beautiful assistant's butt, fix me the trick with the British handcuffs and the ankle chains...And Don Leobar would do it for him. They were both from Durango, that's why Zorak gave him the job."

"Who were the other two friends you mentioned?"

"Gimme another one," said the older man, exiting the conversation and walking, glass in hand, toward the man playing solitaire at the far end of the bar.

"One of them was Zorak's cousin, his bodyguard. A real jerk, he thought he was a big shot, with that forty-five of his..."

"And the other one?"

"His manager, PR man, whatever you call it. Nowadays he's got this joint over on San Juan de Letran...Zorak was their meal ticket...The three of them used to sit around for hours back in the shop, shooting the shit and talking about all the money they'd have when Zorak made it really big, and then, bam, Zorak takes the plunge and they got nothing...The sons of bitches spent a whole week crying and drinking fancy tequila...and do you think they ever offered me a drink? Hell if they did...Have another drink on me, dammit!"

Héctor took the refilled glass. What did another one matter after four or five? The barroom floor started to tilt slightly.

"What's the name of the place on San Juan de Letran?"

"La Fuente de Venus…They've got some goodlooking babes there, that's for sure. Wow…Hey, *compadre*, let's go, I gotta take a leak…" he called out to the older man, and pointed at his crotch.

Héctor walked, drunk and alone, through the Colonia San Rafael. In the midst of his alcohol-induced fog his ideas took on an unusual density, everything was transparent, crystal clear. The problem was—what was it? That was the problem right there, he couldn't connect this clarity with anything real. It was like being incredibly smart but with nothing to think about. He laughed at himself a little bit as he walked in his Maderito maze, past the *taquerías* and the store windows full of shoes and records and toys, through the noise of the crowd. It had gotten dark. A purple aura stained the horizon in the direction of Tacuba. Suddenly Héctor stopped. It occurred to him that he was actually going somewhere in particular, toward a destination, not just walking aimlessly. His drunken rambling was carrying him in the direction of Mendiola's house.

The realization lifted his spirits at the same time that it carried him deeper into the mists of his drunkenness. He smiled from ear to ear and topped it off with a burp. Then he headed down Miguel Schultz toward the funeral home. Mendiola lived on the second floor of a tenement next door to a funeral home, and from the kitchen window you could watch the loading and unloading of the deceased, the comings and goings of hearses, and the fancy floral wreaths, polished coffins with shiny brass fittings, uniformed attendants, teary-eyed men and women clutching at wilted flowers.

Maybe that's what made Mendiola what he was, that and his work as a reporter. When he got fed up with all of it, Mendiola would go to professional wrestling matches and get it all out of his system. For thirty-five pesos' admission he saved himself the cost of a psychiatrist.

That's where Héctor had met him, a couple of years ago, while Héctor was on a case, tailing Mil Máscaras's corner man. Mendiola was there, screaming insults at the top of his lungs (between falls and gouged eyeballs and flying kicks) at the government bureaucrats who bribed him, at the editors who eviscerated his stories and sent him off on humiliating assignments, and at himself for accepting it all. His cries and curses were absorbed into the collective howl inside the arena, harmonizing with those of his fellow spectators, like the elderly woman at his side who shouted ringward: "Kill him, kill him, finish him off! Kill the little faggot!"

It was all fresh in Héctor's mind when his friend's round, swollen face appeared in the doorway.

"Sonofabitch. How you doin'?" The newsman spoke laconically, leading the way back into the tiny apartment, where he collapsed onto a bed littered with books and dirty dishes.

"I'm drunk," said the detective, dropping down onto the bed next to the reporter and knocking a plateful of moldy pork rinds onto the floor.

"I thought you didn't drink."

"I don't. I just get drunk."

"For professional reasons?"

"For professional reasons. In the line of duty."

"Well, okay. Okay okay."

"Okay okay what?" asked Héctor and he started to laugh.

"Getting drunk. I also only drink for professional reasons."

"You're drunk too, Mendiola."

"Completely, Belascoarán. I'm totally shitfaced. But all in the line of duty."

They both started to laugh. The reporter pushed himself onto his feet and went over to the window.

"Look, Belascoarán, a funeral."

Héctor stood up, tripped over a pair of shoes and stumbled to his friend's side.

A funeral procession was forming on the street below.

The shiny black coffin jogged Héctor's memory. "Hey, Mendiola," he said. "You ever hear of a guy named Zorak?"

Chapter III

Zorak

You thought that life was spoils, a treasure for the taking. The country certainly encouraged that kind of ideological excess. Still, it was a treasure for which you had to pay a price: through merciless training, long suffering, gnawing poverty; combined with an overriding sense of patriotism of the pledge-of-allegiance variety, and a hefty dose of brown-nosing, bootlicking, and kowtowing.

You thought all this throughout a career in which myth steadily outpaced reality until it finally obscured it completely. Lies and inventions took the place of real events in your memory until they acquired the status of old and venerated truths, which were, in turn—through time or convenience—displaced by new falsifications.

It was easy enough, then, for you to forget the milk truck you drove through Durango's dusty streets, erasing it completely, once and for all. Just like you expunged your real name with that same precise and pitiless eraser: Arturo Vallespino González. And the public grade school, and the little house in the Colonia Dos Aguas (onto which no one ever built the planned addition—just one more wasted, useless dream). You erased your dad, your mom, and your brothers and sisters. On the other hand, you didn't erase the impression that Hollywood's brief incursion into Durango made on a simple milkman: John Wayne seen leaving his hotel, Robert Mitchum pulling the trigger on a sawed-off shotgun during filming, a whole herd of horses let loose in the city streets, a two-dollar tip received from a cameraman's assistant. All this was allowed to remain in the attic of real and imagined memories. And along with them there, in a far corner, was a fantasy that ended up taking on the full weight of reality. The one where you walk out of a steam bath and bump into Jack Palance. Palance gives you a dirty look and swears at you in English, and you spit on the floor and slap him across the face. You told that story so many times that it became a fixed part of your pseudoreality.

Still, none of this really mattered. What mattered, as time went by, was a balanced diet, plenty of fresh vegetables, and several large glasses of creamy milk every day (a lone vestige of the past).

All that, your second life, began with the Filipino. He came to Durango from San Francisco, fleeing from a crime of passion so terrible its memory would sometimes shatter him like a pane of glass. You met him in a Durango whorehouse, where he liked to follow his feats in bed with a strenuous series of calisthenics, buck naked in the middle of the room.

Who knows how you knew, but you saw there the page on which your destiny was written, and you grabbed it and held on.

The Filipino showed you how to build up your body, how to stretch it and harden it and make it respond to your commands, to tone it, to form it into an efficient and powerful machine.

Life split into two distinct parts: the routine milk deliveries, done every morning at top speed, and the afternoons dedicated to gymnastics and muscle training.

The Filipino enjoyed passing on his art, and you were a good disciple. After the course in gymnastics, you went on to karate, and from there (once again the hand of fate) to the esoteric secrets of the escape artist, magician, and daredevil. The Filipino had once worked as assistant to an Indian contortionist, touring bars and clubs in California, and he knew some unusual and wonderful tricks. So unusual and so wonderful, in fact, that you would spend entire sleepless nights contemplating the subtleties of escape from a sealed coffin, from a straitjacket, or the dangerous motorcycle jump through a ring of fire.

A year and a half passed in strenuous training, and then one day the Filipino disappeared. You got drunk and stayed that way for three days, and the hangover lasted a week. When you finally showed up again at the dairy, you were out of a job; the assistant personnel manager had personally ripped up your time card.

You shut yourself up in your parents' house and refused to talk to anyone. Nobody knew what was wrong with you, not your mother, not your father, not your brothers and sisters. He always was a little strange, they told each other, doesn't drink, won't eat meat, only vegetables, goes running early in the morning, the little faggot never had a girlfriend, no meat, only vegetables, no cigarettes, no booze, *ay hijo mio*, this isn't food you eat, and on and on.

Finally you got a job teaching gymnastics in the local grade school when the regular teacher got sick, and it was there that you discovered your second great talent: you could talk the talk. You'd never known it. You had it in you all along but you never knew it until now. You had your students to thank for that. From the very beginning they had a nickname for you, El Clavillazo, after a television clown, and even today many of them, office workers and factory workers, shopkeepers, policemen, and truck drivers, might remember, if someone were to jog their memory, the gym teacher with the funny way of talking that they'd had once for six months back in grade school, who used to say things like "eggsercises," and "germnastics," and would talk about the importance of staying fit for a better "Meggsico."

El Clavillazo, stupid nickname that it was, was soon relegated to the dustbin of erased memories.

After that you lucked into a job in the Club Laderas del Norte, where the wives of Durango's politicians and captains of industry went for exercise. There you fine-tuned your gift for gab, and took in three thousand pesos a month. That's right, *señora*, see how easy it is to slim up the hips…

A cheap grade school patriotism and the spiel of a housewives' weight loss trainer were the twin elements that would define and enliven your language for the rest of your life. Faithful companions, they would never leave you.

It was at the health club that you gave your first big public performance, churning out six hundred consecutive push-ups without showing signs of fatigue. It was the scene of your first private performance as well: finally, late one afternoon in the locker room, you got laid by the wife of the general manager of Vinícola de Durango, S.A.

In 1967, at the age of twenty-four, you decided that it was time for the final, decisive, most daring leap of all. And you disappeared for an entire month.

Durango died there, forever, and with it, Arturo Vallespino González.

And, in a cheap hotel in Irapuato, Zorak was born—after a lot of back and forth with different names and esoterica. The new name was accompanied by a turban, a blue Mao jacket, white slacks, and a golden cape.

One month to the day after Arturo Vallespino disappeared from Durango, Zorak made his first appearance on national television, live from Mexico City.

If someone today were to say that it was all pure chance, and if you were alive to contradict them, you would tell them about the importance of perseverance and dedication, about the payoff of sweat and hard work. But the fact is, it *was* pure chance, and you aren't here to say otherwise.

Raúl Velasco had an opening in his weekly Sunday extrava-
ganza, and a guy who could do a thousand pushups live on
the air was just what he needed to fill the hole.

And now here in our studios, the incredible Zorak, the
world's greatest bodybuilder and master of mental control.

You came on stage accompanied by four torch bearers and
a slightly cross-eyed but shapely young woman whom Raúl
Velasco had hired to speak for you.

Dr. Zorak has taken a vow of silence and his beautiful
assistant will serve as intermediary.

She explained that you were about to give a small dem-
onstration of the potential of the human body by doing one
thousand push-ups without a break, in front of the studio
audience. She said that you were from Bombay, that you
were not a charlatan but, in fact, a medical doctor who had
advanced to a high level of spiritual development.

And while Raúl Velasco announced that they would be
checking in at regular intervals to observe your progress, and
that the studio audience would serve as witness, you made
an overt display of gathering your concentration, controlling
your breathing, and then went to it.

You were there for almost four hours doing push-ups, and
every fifteen minutes the cameras turned and focused on you.
You and you alone, on national television.

It was your moment of glory. Television is the essence of
home and country, and a live national broadcast is Mexico
itself, one hundred percent. Everything else is a lie. Arturo
Vallespino never appeared on television, therefore he didn't
exist. Zorak was on TV for four hours, during which he was
far more real that the rest of his countrymen. During those
few hours, he become one with Mexico.

And, of course, you did the thousand push-ups.

But it wasn't all easy street. Following that first taste of
glory, which earned you six thousand pesos, after you'd paid

the cross-eyed assistant and the four torch bearers (next time there'd only be two), you couldn't get any more work. You had nothing more to offer and not even Raúl Velasco was interested in bringing you on again for a thousand deep knee bends.

So you took refuge in a fleabag hotel in the Colonia Guerrero to meditate on your situation—this time for real. And there, watching TV all day long, day after day, you began to understand what show business was all about.

A month later you struck a deal with the producers of *The Marathon Show*.

Your cross-eyed assistant became Señorita S, and you embroidered a scarlet Z on the pocket of your Mao jacket, on the turban, and the cape.

The S was originally supposed to be for Soraida, but by the time someone told you that it was actually spelled with a Z, it was too late; you'd already had an S sewn onto her black uniform. There was no turning back, S it was.

This time you escaped from a locked trunk, and the five thousand pesos they paid you all went to the carpenter who made the special trunk for you, and who would make the gadgets for your subsequent performances. That's why you went a week without eating, and not, as one idiot reporter wrote, to prepare yourself mentally for your next feat of magic.

This was the beginning of a career marked by both glory and accident. Second-degree burns suffered while driving a motorcycle through a brick wall covered with burning gasoline; a broken arm during your escape from a locked safe. But this had a special appeal to an audience fed up with untouchable heroes. A hero who came through at the end a little worse for the wear gave the act a sense of real danger, it Mexicanized the spectacle, made the magic more real.

So there you were, wasting your imagination and your balls (more of the latter than the former) on increasingly spectacular feats.

You were stronger, better coordinated, and more confident than ever.

You tempted fate on the high wire, through acts of daring escape, motorcycle jumping, feats of physical resistance (remaining six minutes underwater), fakirism (a forty-day hunger strike, with weekly in-depth televised updates and daily news flashes).

After the hunger strike you married Señorita S. She'd finally decided that her career as a pantyhose model was going nowhere, and that your future could be hers to share.

By 1971 you'd reached the top. You earned good money, and your only worry was to think of some appropriately daring spectacle for next week's performance. You read Houdini and Max Reinbach, Lilibal and Dr. Lao Feng. You added an esoteric touch to your old spiel, derived from the pseudo-Buddhist drivel that Señorita S (whose real name was Márgara) was so fond of. So you called a meeting with Raúl Velasco, and announced that you planned to walk blindfolded across a high wire a hundred and fifty feet above the ground, and that you intended to use that opportunity to speak, in your own voice, for the first time to the television audience.

Of course, he loved the high wire idea, and he loved the blindfold even better. He wasn't too happy about your speaking in public, but he owed it to you, so there wasn't much he could do. And that was how Dr. Zorak broke his vow of silence.

The performance was the *ne plus ultra* in the life of an ex-milkman from Durango. Before the cameras and the nation, you revealed that you were actually Mexican (you didn't reveal your former name, by now you had only one name, crowned with glory: Zorak); and you dedicated the performance to the young people of Mexico, in the hope that they would turn away from drugs, left-wing politics, alcohol, and dancing. You explained that what the country needed was healthy young bodies—and that was the path that you could offer them by your example. Señorita S took the microphone briefly to add that you were the world's number one daredevil and magician, and that you regularly received telegrams from all over the United States (not one) and Europe (one, an offer to perform in a night-club in Madrid).

Two years later you were dead, killed while performing a stunt for the opening of a new housing subdivision. You were hanging suspended in midair below a helicopter when the cable broke and sent you falling to your death. A two-hundred-foot plunge, and your days of glory came to an abrupt end.

You left behind you a pair of innovative daredevil stunts, a name that was briefly commercialized in a new, but never successful, brand of coconut-and-almond cookies, and a comic book series that reached a total of thirty-two issues.

That was your story.

Chapter IV

An exalted mind, a happy heart,
the workday begins, life in the balance.
—*Roy Brown*

The subway's violent motion finally cut through Belascoarán's high, leaving him instead with a dull, persistent headache. At Hidalgo the train was assaulted by an unruly mob of ordinarily peaceful citizens. The horde pushed and squeezed the passengers already inside the car, until Héctor was lifted off the floor, pressed between a pair of office workers and a football player, who lost his helmet and his gym bag in the crush. When they pulled into the Bellas Artes station, the whole thing degenerated into a mass of pushing and shoving bodies, knees and elbows trying to force a gap in the immovable human wall that blocked the car doors. A woman police officer on the platform was pawed by a hundred hands while she shouted repeatedly: *Let the people off before you board!*

This is all the exercise a private detective would ever need, riding the subway a dozen times a day, thought Héctor. It seemed to him that it might not be a bad idea if the national soccer team were to train in the subway a couple of times a week in preparation for the Central American Games.

He walked through the traffic and the neon along San Juan de Letran, enjoying the soft night breeze. The city cast its spell over him even now, despite his headache and the bad taste in his mouth.

La Fuente de Venus hadn't opened yet. Two showgirls, Suzane and Melina, flashed tits and ass from the dozen or so photographs in the glass by the door. One of them was dressed as Cleopatra and surrounded by a group of Roman soldiers (!!). In one picture—to the left and behind a smiling Melina slipping out of a tiny skirt made of little pieces of metal—stood Don Leobardo, complete with toga and helmet, breastplate and spear. Well, that was one mystery solved.

"Real good-lookers, eh boss?" said a man entering the club with a hand truck loaded with soft drink cases.

"Is the owner around? I want to talk to him," said Héctor.

"You looking for someone to set you up with one of the girls? I can't do it for you myself, but I'll tell you what…it's no problem, a thousand pesos gets you whatever you want…They'll even do it dressed up like Cleopatra and everything."

"I've got some business with the owner."

"Salas, Don Agustín? You're too late. He's dead. Somebody killed him."

Héctor crossed the street and set off in the direction of his office. The club would be open in another couple of hours, and right now he needed his chair to do some thinking.

There was a light on in the office. El Gallo sat at his drawing table, deciphering a pile of maps and diagrams. The window was open, and the light from the street fell across the desk and its wrinkled papers.

"What's up, detective?"

"Howya doin'?"

"Carlos the upholsterer asked me to give you a message. He went home a couple of hours ago, when I got here. He said there were these two guys hanging around here all day. Young guys with dark glasses. They came in once and asked for you. You'd better be careful."

Héctor crossed the room slowly and dropped into his chair. He rubbed his eyes with his fists, trying to get his headache to go away.

"What's going on? It all seems pretty confusing to me."

"That about sums it up, Gallo."

Now he had the names of the two dead men, but he didn't know what his connection was to either of them. Why had they sent him the dead body and the photograph of the other one? Better yet, why had they killed them in the first place?

He pushed it all around a few times inside his head:

1. It was a trap, bait. For what? Why?

2. There was some connection between the dead men and himself that he was unaware of.

3. It was all a big mistake.

Maybe there was some connection from the past. It could be…In the middle of his mental haze, an idea started to come together. Perhaps. The two carpenters had mentioned a third man, Zorak's bodyguard. If he wasn't dead by now, like the rest of them, maybe he'd know what was going on. And Zorak, who seemed to be at the crux of the whole bizarre story, had left a widow, Señorita S. That was another loose thread that he could pull on. And then there was the unused airplane ticket. Somebody had paid for it. And whether or not he could find out who, he'd decided to cash it in for the money. It would be a good joke, a little bit of justice.

"Gallo, I'm going to a strip club on San Juan de Letran. I'll be back. If you see anything out of the ordinary, light the lamp on my desk, where I can see it from the street."

"Whatever you say. Do you think there's going to be trouble?"

"You never know. I wouldn't want to take a chance and have someone mistake me for a Roman soldier."

El Gallo laughed and Héctor went back down to the street.

✤ ✤ ✤

"The one and only Melina! She can make men drool until they slip and fall in the puddle at their feet. One look at her and you'll know what I mean, gentlemen. I bring you the swishing, swaying queen of the night: Melina!"

Héctor applauded wildly, taking his cue from the men at the next table. The dimly lit club was filled suddenly by the brash flash of a spotlight. Glasses clinked, a drum rolled.

Melina made her entrance dressed as Cleopatra and escorted by three (not four) Romans. When the enthusiastic cheers of the thirty or forty regulars sitting around the stage died down, the drumroll stopped and Melina took a few steps forward.

"I want to ask for your patience for just a minute, my dear friends—" She was cut off by a new round of cheering. "I need to say something very serious. Something truly serious, and something that has been a terrible shock to us here at La Fuente de Venus. Agustín Salas, the owner of the Fuente, the man who cared so much and helped us in our artistic careers, Don Agustín has passed away." She paused to lick away a tear, then went on, "Don Agustín has passed on to a better life, along with his good friend Don Leobardo, who used to play one of my Romans, just for the simple pleasure of being with us in the show, sharing our joy." She pointed to the three surviving and undoubtedly disconsolate Romans. "And our sorrows. But that's show business, folks. Friends come and go, some find success and others fail, and I'm sure that Don Agustín would have wanted the show to go on." She raised her arms, which brought a renewed cheer from the audience. "So here we go!" There was another drumroll and the Romans took their places.

The lights went down and Héctor took a moment to look around at his fellow revelers. The three men with crooked ties and wavy black hair at the next table over. The two men with briefcases competing for the attention of the miniskirted woman who sat coyly between them. Who were they? Bureaucrats? Cops? And if they were cops, were they from the secret police, the auxiliary police, the judicial police, the special, the bank, the preventive, the traffic, the federal? Merchants from the Merced? Loan sharks? Upholsterers, butchers, auto parts dealers? Grocers? Small-time drug dealers? Grifters? Mechanics? Chauffeurs?

At the end of her Cleopatra routine, Melina removed her jeweled crown and threw it into the audience. She'd taken off the rest of her costume sometime earlier. The lights came up again, and a trio of waiters attacked the tables with fresh bottles of watered-down whiskey, watered-down black market cognac, cheap Mexican brandy, and rum.

"Who owns the place now?" Héctor asked one of the waiters.

"Who knows? Maybe one of Don Agustín's cousins. Nobody's told us anything. They just said to keep working, that's it…"

"What about the other guy who was friends with Don Agustín and Leobardo, their pal from their old Zorak days?" Héctor insisted, holding on to the waiter's sleeve to keep him from getting away.

"You mean Captain Freshie? He hasn't shown his face around here in days."

"What's Captain Freshie's real name?"

The waiter jerked his arm free. "Ask Melina. He used to be after her ass."

In the meantime, the stripper had started a new routine. Dressed in a long, low-cut dress, with an enormous yo-yo in her hand, she led the audience in singing along: "Melina, let me play with your yo-yo-yo, Melina let me play with your yo-yo-yo."

The audience picked up the refrain. Melina tried to get the giant yo-yo to go up and down while she marked out a few awkward dance steps.

"It'll cost you a hundred," said the waiter, returning to Héctor's side.

The detective put down his bottle of soda. "What will?"

"Captain Freshie just showed up."

Héctor pulled two wrinkled fifty-peso notes from his pocket and passed them to the waiter, who turned his back to Héctor and said in a low voice, "That's him, over there, by the door with the red light."

Héctor looked in the direction the waiter indicated. Illuminated by a soft red bulb, a man of about forty leaned against the backstage door, his eyes on the stripper. He had a thick mustache and wore a black suit with a white necktie. He lit a cigarette. Héctor stood up and called the waiter over to pay his bill. Melina finished her number, teasing the men seated in front of the stage with the bobbing yo-yo. Captain Freshie glanced distractedly around the room, and his eyes met Héctor's. His face changed, a line of tension deepening around his mouth. He threw his cigarette to the floor and went through the door behind him, glancing quickly over his shoulder at the detective. Héctor picked up his change and started to push his way across the crowded floor.

The door gave onto a long, poorly lit hallway, a pair of doors on either side and a gray-metal door at the far end. One of the side doors opened and the club's other stripper came out into the hallway. She was naked except for a tall peacock feather headdress. She stared at Héctor.

"Have you seen Captain Freshie?"

"Never heard of him."

Héctor squeezed by her. She lowered her head and shook her feathers in his face.

The gray-metal door opened on an empty parking lot. The air was warm, at least as warm as inside the club. A drunk was trying to ride a bicycle. He would kick at the pedal a couple of times and fall over. Then get up and do it again. There was no one else. Captain Freshie had disappeared.

Héctor yawned, lit a cigarette, decided to go back to his office and get some sleep.

It must have been after two A.M. The street, strangely empty, glowed under the neon lights. A couple of cars stopped at the light, and he crossed placidly in front of them. He was out for a walk. Just a little stroll at two in the morning through a hot, deserted city. He tried in vain to keep his mind blank, open to the impressions of the night, but two images hemmed him in: the dark body of the woman with the peacock feather headdress, and the rabbit pissing on his rug at home. He'd better bring him something to eat first thing in the morning.

Chapter V

...we are time and in time we exist like
smoke in the air, like the fleeting air itself.
—Roberto Fernández Retamar

After wading through the obligatory red tape, he was finally able to cash in the plane ticket to New York for a wad of thousand-peso bills, which he held tightly in his hand inside his jacket pocket. Now the joke was on them. He could keep the money as a sort of advance toward his search for Don Agustín's and Don Leobardo's killers. Or he could simply give it away to the first person he saw on the street. Like that guy there…Héctor stopped to watch a street vendor walking along under the weight of three heavy wooden ladders; the man stared hopefully back at the detective, more interested in the possibility of actually getting rid of one of the ladders than in the money the sale would bring him. Or how about that one: a secretary quickened her pace to keep up with her busy schedule.

He walked across the tree-lined Alameda, a light breeze cooling his skin and kicking up puffs of dirt here and there as it picked up force. He stopped in front of a hand-lettered sign announcing a campaign to collect a kilometer of coins for the literacy campaign in the new Nicaragua, and laid down his several thousand pesos in bills before the astonished high school student who stood guard over one end of the chain of money.

Then the detective turned and fled, running from his own embarrassment at the look of admiration on the student's face.

✢ ✢ ✢

"Just because you've got a gun and you call yourself a detective, that doesn't mean you get to drink the last soda pop. Not around here. No way," said Gilberto Gómez Letras.

"We believe in democracy," said Carlos the upholsterer.

Héctor crossed his arms and smiled. "So what do you want to do, flip a coin?"

It was pouring rain. Dark clouds scudded over the city, tree limbs blew down, the puddles were choked with dead leaves. A cold wind threw the rain against the window. Scattered splotches of light shone through the wet glass from the first lights coming on in the office building across the street.

"I'll tell you what. If you guys make the run, I'll treat you to a couple of *cafés con leche* in exchange for the soda pop," proposed the detective.

"And go out in this fucking weather? You're off your rocker."

"It's raining like a son of a bitch," said the upholsterer.

"Who you calling a son of a bitch?" asked the plumber.

"Suck me," countered Carlos, displaying a small tack between his two front teeth and pointing with two fingers of one hand at his crotch.

"Okay, so we flip a coin," Héctor interrupted them.

The last soft drink sat impassive and alone on the dust-covered desktop. It seemed to enjoy being the center of attention.

"Whoever wins the soda goes for coffee," offered Gilberto as a compromise.

So that was it. They didn't want the soda at all. They wanted him to go out for the coffee. Couple of shysters, thought Héctor.

"I'll have a *café con leche* and a couple of sweet rolls," said the upholsterer.

Héctor got up and roamed around the room, while Carlos went back to rhythmically tapping small tacks into an over-stuffed armchair. He held the tacks in his mouth, transferring them one by one to the magnetized head of his hammer, then tapping them into the wood while he stretched the fabric tight with his other hand. Gilberto the plumber, on break for the last hour, sat watching from Héctor's worn-out swivel chair, fascinated by the other craftsman's art.

"There'll be cobwebs growing on that chair before I go out in this rain to get coffee for you guys. And anyway, the Chink who runs the place doesn't let you take out the cups."

"That's because you won't leave a deposit," said the plumber.

Héctor dropped into the leather armchair they'd had since they first moved into the office. The springs bulged, the wood groaned.

"Don't you think it's time you did a little work on this thing?" he asked Carlos.

"Nope. I'm an anarchist," said the bearded upholsterer enigmatically.

Héctor stretched his arms over his head, feeling his fatigue, the sense of protection that the warm office gave him with the storm outside, letting himself go. He lit another cigarette.

The office consisted of one large room with a scarred wood floor and dirty, cream-colored walls. A topless Meche Carreño looked out from one corner. A photo of Emiliano Zapata (an accusatory stare, on the verge of tears for the country that was slipping from his hands) hung over a dilapidated desk heaped with plumber's tools and parts, lengths of rusty pipe, broken faucets. Héctor's desk was surprisingly empty of papers, except for a single old newspaper that did triple duty as address book, notebook, and phone memo pad. El Gallo's drawing table stood unoccupied, while a random assortment of furniture in various stages of disrepair filled every available bit of remaining space. The floor, unswept for at least a month, was a disaster area of dirt and dust, piles of sawdust, grease, and lumps of furniture stuffing.

And, outside, the storm. The delicious, driving deluge that would shake him out of this impasse. Break the tie score in this weird opponentless match of the last two days.

Héctor Belascoarán Shayne, a private detective for strange and revolutionary reasons, was a rider on the storm. Or at least that's what he decided to be on that rainy afternoon. He got up from the chair and announced: "You win. I'll go get the coffee."

"Don't put yourself out on my account," said the plumber Gilberto Gómez Letras. "Heavy on the milk, two donuts."

"Here we go again," said Carlos the upholsterer.

Héctor put a green windbreaker over his sweater and tied the hood tight under his chin. He lit another cigarette.

"Don't you ever do any work?" he asked the plumber.

"I'm, you know, I'm one of them whatchamacallits…"

"What?"

"You know, same as him," he said, pointing at Carlos.

"Anarchists," smiled the upholsterer.

It was raining hard enough to make anyone want to skip work, anarchist or no. Mud on the sidewalk, oily rainbows in the puddles. Passing cars threw huge, arching jets of water over the curb, covering store windows with a brownish torrent that was immediately washed away again by the dense unbroken waves of pounding rain.

He jumped puddles, dodged a Volkswagen, and hurried through the door of the Chinese restaurant.

"Don Jelónimo," he said, imitating the proprietor's Chinese accent. "Coffee for my two officemates."

The Chinaman shot him an unfriendly look. First, because he called him Jelónimo, and second, because he refused to pay a deposit on the coffee cups. Héctor sat in a booth next to a newspaper vendor come in out of the rain. He bought a copy of *Ovaciones.*

"Want to go for a ride in the rain?"

Héctor looked up from the headlines to find the woman with the ponytail standing before him in a bright red slicker, shiny with raindrops. He got up and followed her out, ignoring the Chinaman, who shouted after him to pay for the unclaimed coffee.

They got into a red Renault. She started the engine without looking at him, and pulled out into the driving rain. The windshield wipers beat crazily back and forth. She turned on the radio. The deejay was explaining the difference between the blues and Dixieland. Then he introduced a piece by Mingus. Héctor looked at her out of the corner of his eye. What was it that connected him so strongly to this woman? They'd known each other for two years, since the beginning of Belascoarán's career as a detective, when he was hunting down a strangler and she was searching for a spectacular way to die. Their love for each other came and went in waves, and neither of them could ever tell how long each new phase would last. They'd even lived together for brief periods of time, when they were both able to break through the shell of their highly valued solitude. A couple of months earlier, irresistibly attracted to each other's aura of madness, they'd actually begun to entertain the possibility of a stable relationship. But it was too much for her, and she'd packed up and fled.

The car turned onto Reforma at Morelos, throwing up a curtain of water on both sides.

"How's the rabbit?" she asked suddenly.

"I like it," answered Héctor.

He took a cloth from the glove compartment and tried to wipe the steam off the windshield. The noise of the rain on the roof of the car made a good accompaniment to Mingus.

Only a few cars could be seen driving along Reforma; it was as if the rest had been dissolved by the rain.

"What are you working on these days?"

"It's a strange story…a guy dressed up like a Roman soldier in a movie shows up dead in my office bathroom. Then they send me a picture of another corpse, and a plane ticket to New York."

She smiled.

"We're going to have to stop seeing each other for a while," she said.

"We're going to do what we always do, without ever agreeing on anything, and if we're lucky it'll turn out all right in the end," he said.

As they rounded the traffic circle at the Ángel de la Independencia, another car swerved in front of the Renault, forcing the woman with the ponytail to cut the wheel sharply, and sending them skidding across the flooded avenue.

"Son of a bitch," she said, dropping down into second before picking up speed again.

"Take it easy, I think that was on purpose," said Héctor, taking out his gun and holding it between his legs.

"Don't be paranoid, detective. It's just some asshole who doesn't know how to drive in the rain. He wants to show how macho he is. Only problem is he doesn't know who he's fooling with."

She accelerated behind the other car, made as though she were going to pass on the left, then put her foot to the floor and darted past them on the right side, with her hand on the horn.

A second later, a bullet shattered the driver's-side rear window.

"Who's paranoid now?" said Héctor.

"Take it easy, detective, it's just some macho Mexican trying to get his frustrations out."

Héctor tried to look back through the steamed-up rear window. Rain fell on the back seat.

"What kind of car were they driving? How many were there?"

"Two, I think."

"Did you see their faces?"

"You think I could see anything in this rain? It was an old Ford."

She pushed the car faster and turned to the left at Sevilla. Héctor turned to see if he could spot the Ford behind them. It followed thirty yards back, a faded yellow Ford.

"Still there?" she asked.

"A yellow Ford?"

"That's them."

She crossed Chapultepec at the yellow light, then pulled over to the side and stopped.

"What do you want to do, lose them or find them?" she asked.

"I'd like to follow them."

"That's not going to be easy. They'll recognize our car."

"Then—"

"Let me at least put a little scare into them," she said.

"Oh, swell. Nothing like going for a nice drive on a rainy day."

The woman with the ponytail smiled. "You're the detective. Me, I like to drive. They can cut me off or drive me off the road, but nobody shoots at me."

She pulled out just as the light turned green at the intersection behind them, then turned onto Durango, watching for the yellow Ford to appear in her rear-view mirror before picking up speed.

At Sonora, she slammed on the breaks, skidding, and then pulled into a parking lot. She threw the car into reverse and turned around. At sixty miles per hour she headed the wrong way down Durango straight at the yellow Ford.

"What the hell are you doing?" shouted Héctor. "We're going to hit them head on."

"How much you want to bet they chicken out first?" she said with a grin. She smashed her foot down on the accelerator pedal even harder.

The driver of the yellow Ford suddenly saw the Renault speeding toward him. In desperation, he spun the wheel to the side and ran the car onto the median strip and into a palm tree.

The Renault went by with its horn blaring.

There were two of them. And they were scared to death, thought Héctor.

"That's why I love you. Because you're crazy," he said.

"I think it would be better if we didn't see each other for a while."

"I could use a good driver like you," said the detective.

"Whenever you want."

Héctor stretched out his hand and placed it on her leg, her black jeans.

"It'll never work out, detective," she said.

"Didn't we know that all along?"

The woman with the ponytail pointed the car toward the Colonia Roma. It was around eleven at night when the red Renault stopped in front of Héctor's office. The detective caressed her face once and got out.

"Are you sure you don't want to come and sleep at my place?"

"Yeah. I've got some stuff to do here, and later on I've got to go over to the Fuente de Venus."

She smiled. It had stopped raining. The street was full of puddles and mud and wet newspapers.

Héctor went up in the elevator, thinking that he'd never made it back with the donuts and coffee. They'd never let him live it down, either.

El Gallo was at work at his drawing table.

"Did Gilberto and Carlos go home?"

"They left you a note under that bottle of soda."

The note said that the bottle had been poisoned with "the stuff plumbers use to unclog drains."

Héctor took the bottle and opened it with the barrel of his .45.

"Very cool," said El Gallo, with admiration.

Héctor drank the soda with gusto.

"Have you ever driven at seventy-five miles an hour the wrong way down a street head on at another car?"

"What did the other car do?"

"Swerved into a palm tree."

"They must have been shitting in their pants."

"Well, I couldn't exactly see from where I was sitting, but I'd say it'd be a good bet they had their assholes shrunk up to about this big," said the detective, holding up his hand to make a tiny space between his index finger and his thumb.

He kicked off his shoes and went over to the window. The street was deserted.

"If I go to sleep, will you wake me up when you leave in the morning?"

"Is six o'clock all right?"

"Perfect," said the detective, collapsing into the armchair.

So now they wanted to kill him too, or at least scare him off. And he'd never made it back with the coffee and donuts for Gilberto and Carlos, and she drives better than the Rodríguez brothers ever did—before they crashed—he thought as he drifted off to sleep.

Chapter VI

An Intimate Portrait of Héctor Belascoarán Shayne's Three Officemates

First examine the neighborhood
before you choose your dwelling.
—*Chinese Proverb*

Basic Facts

Gilberto Gómez Letras has the unpleasant habit of picking his nose with the little finger of his right hand. Since his hands are usually covered with grease, he carries the mark of his vice on his cheek.

Carlos Vargas, the upholsterer, made First Communion three times, because "each time they gave you a suit and a pair of shoes."

When El Gallo Villareal was fifteen, he had a girlfriend who died in the same plane crash that killed Institutional Revolutionary Party chairman Carlos Madrazo and the tennis star Rafael Osuna.

Gilberto was expelled from the third grade (at the Aquiles Serdán School in the Colonia Álamos) for stealing the faucet handles from the girls' rest room and the toilet floats from the faculty rest room.

For two full years Carlos the upholsterer lived surrounded by television sets, car stereos, washing machines, console stereos, and refrigerators, all bought from door-to-door salesmen on the installment plan. He didn't have any furniture, but his house was full of electrical appliances and gadgets, "so as not to feel any worse off than the next son of a bitch."

Sometimes (on rainy afternoons) El Gallo takes in a triple feature at some small neighborhood movie house, preferably Tarzan films or Westerns. He doesn't buy any sandwiches or popcorn or soda, he just sits there and watches the whole six and a half hours without ever taking his eyes off the screen.

Gilberto was born in Michoacán and came to live in Mexico City when he was six.

Carlos Vargas was born in Mexico City, in the Colonia Morelos, near Tepito.

El Gallo was born in Chihuahua and came to Mexico City for the first time when he received a scholarship to study engineering at the Politécnico.

FAMOUS SAYINGS

If they're going to suck me off tomorrow, they might as well go ahead and suck me off today. —*Carlos Vargas*

Any rational evaluation of the future efficiency of the work in question must not fail to consider the fact that the supervising engineer was eating a chicken and mole sandwich when he drew up the original plans; the resulting dark stain (see grid 161-b) is without a doubt the reason why the toilets frequently overflow in the Colonia Aviación Civil. —*Javier Villareal, civil engineer (from a report that once cost him his job)*

The best *taquerías* are always run by guys who get laid a lot. Don't ask me why, some things you just can't explain. —*Gilberto Gómez Letras*

Guadalajara en un llano, and around here we just take it in the rear. —*Carlos Vargas*

I'd better do it the way I told you because that's the way I thought it, and I only think things once, because afterward they just kind of slip my mind. —*Gilberto Gómez Letras (from a telephone conversation with a customer about a broken pipe)*

Lucky for you I'm as slow as I am. Otherwise I'd already have been married, gotten divorced, turned queer, gone straight again, and remarried. —*Javier Villareal (from a conversation with his girlfriend)*

To succeed in life you don't necessarily have to have a big dick. But you do need some decent clothes, for instance. —*Gilberto Gómez Letras*

BASIC FACTS

When Gilberto picks his nose, he turns his finger back and forth in a circular motion, with a certain expertise peculiar to the task. The result of his labors is then rolled into a ball and flicked into a corner of the room.

Carlos Vargas has pictures from each of his three first Communions.

El Gallo Villareal still has a letter from his girlfriend from when he was fifteen, the one in the plane crash.

Gilberto keeps his money in a giant piggy bank shaped like a professional wrestler. When he fills up three of them, he plans to buy himself a piece of land out by El Molinito. This is the third time he's started saving, after first winning the wrestler-piggy banks at a local street fair. The other two times he had to break them open before he'd filled all three. The first time was to pay for his mother's funeral, and the second time was when he ran off to Veracruz for a week with a couple of prostitutes. The wrestler (with yellow mask and cape) sits on top of his television set, where his children treat it with a greater reverence than the various religious images with which it shares that pedestal.

A year ago Carlos Vargas tried to get a job at the Ford auto plant near Mexico City. He'd heard that they paid a good wage in the seat upholstery section, and he was attracted by the security of a steady job, the benefits, and the idea of a whole factoryful of workers (sometimes he gets bored working alone). And he was excited about the chance to do some union organizing. He passed all the tests, but he couldn't fool the company psychologist, who detected in him something out of the ordinary: a mixture of stubborn nonconformism and authentic professional pride. He couldn't picture him as a docile cog on the assembly line, so he decided to reject his application, even though there was no objective reason to do so.

El Gallo Villareal has a sweet roll and a soda pop for breakfast every day. For El Gallo, the introduction of canned soda pop was an extraordinary technological advance, allowing him to eat his breakfast while he walks home from work. He leaves the office around seven in the morning and walks the streets of the city center with a bagful of sweet rolls in one hand and a can of Pepsi in the other. He likes to stop in front of the twin churches of La Santa Veracruz, where he finishes his breakfast surrounded by pigeons. He gives the crumbs to the pigeons and then takes the bus home to the Colonia San Rafael.

Gilberto Gómez Letras once dreamed of opening up a used-car lot. His other dream jobs have included doorman in a luxury apartment building, owner of a welding shop, quality-control manager in a gin distillery, and manager of a brothel in Zihuatanejo. Instead, he's worked in a plastics factory, for a bathroom fittings manufacturer, and as a plumber's assistant.

El Gallo loves bossa nova and samba. He never misses a concert, and he's got every record ever put out in Mexico by Jobim, Edu Lobo, Laurindo Almeida, Vinicius de Moraes, Badem Powel, Stan Getz, Chico Buarque de Holanda, Joao Gilberto, Carlos Lyra, Luiz Bonfa, Charlie Byrd, and Marcos Valle. And he dreams about Astrud Gilberto. He'd like to live with her in an isolated house (which he's drawn the plans for and sketched out dozens of times) in Baja California, near Cabo San Lucas. The house's distinguishing characteristics are all acoustic: the constant low roar of the breakers on the rocks, and a stereo system with enormous speakers in every room. In his dreams, he's having breakfast with Astrud Gilberto in a very large, entirely white kitchen. He's wearing a cream-colored pajama, and she has on a yellow camisole. They're both barefoot; the gray light of a sunless day filters in through the window.

SELF-PORTRAITS: CARLOS VARGAS

If they come at me from the front, I'll give it to them straight on. But around here, they always hit you from the side, or they stick it to you from behind.

That's what made me change myself, to put them off their guard, so that they wouldn't ever know what I was up to, so that…

I don't even like the music, but I've got a shitload of *ranchera* records under my bed, Negrete, Pedro Infante, Aceves Mejía, Cuco Sánchez, that whole crowd. Just to throw them off. Or, who knows. I've also got two black leather jackets, the kind that everybody was wearing around '69–'70. The way it works is that sometimes I make fools out of them, sometimes I make a fool out of myself, and sometimes I just end up taking it in the rear. That's how it's been lately. Or just about always. When I was born, in 1946, my dad immediately thought to himself: "Here is a son to learn my trade and earn money for the family"; I'm sure he was already thinking it when they took me and laid me on my mother's breast for the first time, before they'd even given me a name, a little newborn baby. Because that's the way it is in the Morelos, you're born with your fate already laid out for you. Later on you can take your fate and change it, but not because you're any tougher than anybody else; it just turns out that parents are rotten fortune-tellers. If my folks had to make a living predicting the future, they'd die of starvation. That's the only reason I became an upholsterer instead of a shoemaker, or some other trade. They made me this way, I didn't do it myself. They made me quit school after the sixth grade, and they made it so I never trusted anybody; and it was from them that I inherited my small hands and soft skin that kept me from becoming a boxer. Because of them. Later on I made myself different. The normal thing was always just to get tougher as you got older. Me, I made myself different, and I learned to get along, but I also learned how to change. I went out drinking with the guys, and I went to the whorehouses and all that, but I also read encyclopedias, and books about Freud, the ones they sell at the newsstands on the street. And I got as much out of it as I could, and that was where I started to understand this thing about how they're always trying to make you one way, and you're trying to make yourself into something else. That's why I'm always changing jobs or getting fired. That's why I joined the union, and became an organizer, and slept out on the ground with the strikers. And that's what got me sent to jail too, and not for ripping somebody off, which would have been the normal thing from where I come from…Sometimes I think I really am my own boss, that my work belongs to me, and my tools, and the books I buy every time I get paid for a job, and my crazy ideas…Sometimes I'm positive that the only thing that really belongs to me is the right to say no, no I won't sell out, no I don't like it, no I won't stand for any more. I've been fired three times in twelve years from jobs in factories and other people's shops, and all that belongs to me too. I swear, sometimes I think that if I didn't like people as much as I do, I'd bash them all over the head with a hammer, all of them. Starting with myself.

BASIC FACTS

El Gallo leads a double life, or rather, a life split in two. He works nights in the office, calculating flow levels and reviewing sewer expansion plans. In the morning he goes home to sleep. In the afternoon he studies psychology at the university. That's where he met his girlfriend. It's not clear whether he stays in school out of a real interest in clinical psychology or a fondness for the open spaces and greenery of the campus. At first it seemed like a good idea. Now, more than anything, it's become a habit.

Gómez Letras frequently leaves work in the middle of the afternoon and goes to a nearby cantina called El Mirador. When the bartender sees him coming through the swinging double doors, he pours out a double tequila anejo. Just like that, without even having to ask.

Carlos Vargas has a scar on his head. Not very big, about an inch and a half long. They hit him on the head with a hammer. They were waiting for him just inside the shop door. It cost his boss almost nothing to have it done: a couple of bottles of rum and a slap on the back. And after the beating, they fired him, so he never was able to organize anything in that rotten little shop after all. Now the scar itches just before it rains.

El Gallo Villareal once stayed drunk for six months. When he was around fifteen, he acquired a taste—partly as a dare and partly as the consequence of a poorly trained palate—for Don Pancho brand liqueurs, especially the crème de menthe, crème de banana, and tangerine. After a couple of parties in which he cleaned out his parents' modest liquor cabinet, he was forced to raise relatively large amounts of cash every week washing cars, making runs to the supermarket, saving his allowance, and mooching off his grandparents, in order to maintain his vice. The sudden, exorbitant consumption of Don Pancho (eighty-six proof) at the Villareals' was grist for the rumor mill in his comfortable, middle-class neighborhood: some said his father was fooling around behind his mother's back, driving her to drink; others insisted that Don Pancho was an aphrodisiac; or that it made delicious cakes…His six-month binge was carried on both in public, drinking with his gang of friends, and in private, drinking alone in vacant lots, crashed out in the back of his older brother's car, or in his room, full of posters of American baseball players. It cost him his girlfriend and his first year of high school.

Gilberto Gómez Letras always fudges the numbers when he bills his clients. It's a compulsion for him, an irresistible necessity. He can never allow himself to add a column of numbers properly. More than just a habit, this systematic, Pythagorean fraud is central to his sense of morality.

Javier Villareal always dresses in a sort of uniform: blue jeans, checked shirt, brown leather jacket. It's a way of establishing his identity as a northerner, a stranger to Mexico City, a way of marking himself as an outsider, a provincial, in a city in which everything becomes the same, a city that wipes out all differences.

Carlos Vargas is a connoisseur of chewing gums. There isn't a brand he isn't familiar with, and he judges them all with the aplomb and expertise of a true gourmet.

Neither Carlos, Gilberto, nor El Gallo voted in the last election.

SELF-PORTRAITS: EL GALLO

I'm really only good for simple things. Like riding a horse in a Marlboro ad. But Marlboros taste like shit, so not even that. In my case, the system broke down. I could have been a hell of an engineer; I might not have known a whole lot about anything else, but I'd have made a great engineer. Not like now. They tell me I've lost my ambition. But how are you going to learn to be a good engineer if the cops suddenly take over your school one day, start shooting everywhere, and poke out your friend's eye with an iron spike rolled up inside a newspaper? That's no way to learn engineering, and I don't give a shit if we'd been on strike and had the whole place shut down for ninety-six days. Besides, what'd they ever have to offer me? Not like the pigeons that eat the breadcrumbs at La Santa Veracruz. Nothing like that. But I did get something out of it: fear, fear of my country, fear of power, fear of the system. And I lost something too: the ability to remain innocent, stupid, pure. My girlfriend says that's why I stay in school. She says I don't give a damn about psychology, but that what I want is to feel like a student again, to go back to being young again. Belascoarán, on the other hand, says that what it is is that, being from the north, I'm naturally drawn to the campus, with its esplanades and open space, which is the closest you can get in this city to the flatlands of La Laguna, or the great, wide open expanses of Chihuahua. Carlos has his own explanation; he says that, according to Freud, the reason I stay in school is that I secretly hope that the cops come back (it was in the Casco de Santo Tomás, it was night, there was a blackout, the street was dark, everything frozen by the incredible sound of the sirens), and that this time, instead of running like a pansy I'll stand my ground and grab a knife and kick some ass. Gilberto Gómez Letras says that's where the babes are, so, naturally. I like everyone's explanation, and in a way I wish they were all partly true. This is what psych has done for me, it helps me to look at everyone else's reasoning and make it pass for my own. My mother says that I just never grew up and that I don't have the right temperament. The fact is that the pigeons in the plaza of La Santa Veracruz couldn't give a shit if I have the right temperament, as long as I bring them breadcrumbs.

FAMOUS SAYINGS

It's not that Javier Solís has a good voice, it's the way he puckers his lips when he sings. —*Gilberto Gómez Letras*

You didn't really think it was that easy, did you? Go back and do it again, and if it comes out all right this time, then you'll know it was luck all along. —*Carlos Vargas*

It isn't the pissing that matters, it's how much foam you make. —*Carlos Vargas*

A great blueprint is as good as a great novel, you just have to know how to read it. —*Javier Villareal*

I should have been a secretary. —*Gilberto Gómez Letras*

BASIC FACTS

Gilberto was operated on twice for appendicitis. The first time was a wrong diagnosis: "woops, just a hernia." The second time was the real thing. Nothing was explained to him very clearly either time, so to this day he swears that human beings have two appendixes. He ought to know.

Carlos has a deeply ingrained fear of glue. Years ago he worked in a shop where all the carpenters sniffed glue. They would get high and spend hours lying underneath their work benches, sunk inside the drug's sickly dreamspace. Carlos always kept his distance from their part of the shop, overcome with a mixture of fear and pity for the three master carpenters and their assistant.

El Gallo is a fanatical baseball fan. His favorite team: the Unión Laguna. But despite his enthusiasm, and the fact that he follows the season closely from start to finish, and holds impassioned discussions with Gilberto (the only one in the office who'll pay him any attention), he's never seen a single game, not even on television. Occasionally he'll go so far as to listen to a game on the radio. In this way he's formed a magical relation with the sport, turning baseball into a part of his private reality. El Gallo himself suspects that real bats and balls and strikes and slides into second and squeeze plays and diamonds and pop-ups don't have much in common with the way he imagines them to be: a completely private reality.

Carlos lives alone in an enormous and decrepit apartment behind the Opera Cinema. The apartment was passed on to him by a friend, a retired professional wrestler who went away to start a pig farm in Michoacán, leaving Carlos his trophies and photographs and other mementos of his profession. Sometimes one of the waitresses from the sea-food restaurant on Hidalgo climbs the stairs and goes to bed with him, and Carlos, all one hundred twenty-two pounds of him, strips down and poses for her under the knowing gaze of the heroes of the ring, and he does the camel clutch and the full nelson on her, the cradle and the sleeper hold, the atomic kneedrop, the two of them in bed.

Gilberto's father passed away two years ago, El Gallo's father is mayor of Saltillo, and Carlos's dad is a seventy-year-old blind shoemaker.

The three of them agree in their love of soda pop, and hot chocolate and donuts.

SELF-PORTRAITS: GILBERTO

They must think that I still want to make it big, that I'm still thinking big. But that's just a front. I know, and they know too, that I'm never going to hit the big time. I've already gotten as far as I'm ever going to get. Sometimes I think I'm already old, worn out. Sometimes I think that it's not so bad the way things are going. Last month I got away with charging this condo on Doctor Balmis triple what they really owed me; I balled a housewife in Polanco, and then the servant in the house next door; I got good and drunk twice; I beat the shit out of this guy whose kids beat up on my kids; I did a helluva job on this one bathroom installation on Parral Street; I visited my mom's grave; I bought myself a black-and-white-checked sport coat; I dreamed I was making it with Irma Serrano; I bought my wife a new record player; I taught one of my daughters how to add; I didn't pay any taxes; I almost saw a dead Roman with his throat cut in the bathroom at the office...

It's all right. Maybe I haven't made it, but I don't have to lick anybody's boots to put food on the table, I've got friends I'd give my life for, I sleep with whoever I want to and I don't have to answer to anybody about it, I don't owe anything. After all, this is Mexico, *cabrones*...And let's face it, I'm an irresponsible bum.

Chapter VII

Our luck has turned,
the light's come on and the chaos is revealed.
—*Francisco Urondo*

It seemed as though life was stuck in a continuous loop of nights and dawns. Nights, with tired feet tripping to the city's nonstop beat, dawns full of harsh light and a sense of uneasiness. While the elevator rattled down the six floors to the street and El Gallo hummed a *ranchera*, Héctor decided the time had come to push the story forward, to force things into the open. Hammer away until the killers had a face and a shape, or at least a motive. What did Zorak have to do with all this, six years after his death? He fascinated Héctor. He had just the right dose of a uniquely Mexican type of glory. A glory bordering on the ridiculous: ephemeral, commercialized, prostituted.

An army of paper delivery boys milled around in front of the doorway to the building. Some were busy folding in the day's supplements, others tied up bundles with string or traded bundles back and forth, and others consulted grimy notepads full of numbers and illegible script.

Héctor raised his arms over his head and stretched. El Gallo, at his side, stifled a yawn, and stuck his hands into his jacket pockets.

Two men moved away from the soda cooler in the restaurant across the street. Their movement caught Héctor's eye. The sun was barely up, and their dark sunglasses were like a warning signal that shook him awake. Instinctively, he raised his hand to his gun in the shoulder holster under his arm.

One of the men had on a worn-out gray suit and a blue shirt; the other one, his greasy hair uncombed, wore a blue plastic raincoat. They both had their hands in their coat pockets.

"Get out of the way," Héctor said to El Gallo when the two men took out their guns. They were twelve yards away, coming toward them across the street, dodging paperboys loaded down with stacks of today's news.

El Gallo smiled at Héctor and it wasn't until he noticed the gun in his hand that he turned sharply to see what was the matter. A paperboy, with a three-foot stack of papers loaded on the back of his bicycle, pedaled in front of Héctor. His balance was precarious and Héctor pushed him off and grabbed the bicycle by the rope that held the papers in place.

The first shot hit the stack of papers. Thousands of words flew in all directions, leaving the smell of fresh ink in the air. El Gallo separated himself from Héctor, and a long-barreled Colt revolver appeared in his hand. The bicycle wobbled and fell over, and Héctor let himself be pulled down behind it. As he fell he sighted down the barrel of his gun toward the belly of the greasy-haired man, but he hesitated as a woman crossed his line of vision carrying a small boy in one arm and a stack of papers under the other. A second bullet ricocheted off the pavement, leaving a hole in Héctor's jacket. The paper hawkers ran for cover, and the gray-suited man was left in the open in the middle of the street. Another shot sounded. Héctor fired at the same time and the man clutched his stomach with both hands. The detective fired again. Blood spurted from the man's chest and he fell over backward. Three yards to the right, greasy head lost a precious second watching his partner go down. When he turned back to locate Héctor, a piece of his jaw exploded and his face became a bloody grimace. Héctor hadn't had time to fire. El Gallo stood behind a *La Prensa* pickup truck, smoke curling from the end of his revolver. Shouts and cries filled the street as the echo of gunshots faded. The screaming had started when the first shots were fired, but Héctor hadn't heard it, only the sound of the shots, and the soft hum of the freely spinning bicycle wheel behind which he'd taken cover.

Suddenly, a silence descended, and the only sound was from the traffic a block away on Bucareli. Then someone started to clap, and others joined in. Surrounded by applause, Héctor approached the two bodies, while El Gallo covered him, like a gunman out of the novels of Marcial Lafuente Estefanía, squeezing the Colt in both his hands.

They were both dead. One of the men stared skyward through his dark glasses, his two hands still trying to plug up the hole in his stomach. The other bullet had probably hit him in the heart; he lay in a huge pool of blood. Héctor took off the dark glasses and stared into his lifeless black eyes. The other man's face was a bloody mess. Héctor checked his pockets. Just a few pesos and an ID card from the subway police. It was the same for the other one. Héctor had blood on his hands, and he wiped them off on the dead man's pants leg. The crowd of paper vendors gathered around, ignoring the detective's .45 and El Gallo's Colt, forming a circle with Héctor and the two corpses at its center and El Gallo, still aiming over the *La Prensa* pickup, at its periphery. Now that the shooting was over they seemed entirely unafraid. Maybe because this was their stock-in-trade, just another story for tomorrow's paper; maybe because blood flowed every few days anyway between Donato Guerra and Bucareli, in knife fights, fist fights, fights with broken bottles; or maybe because they'd decided that Héctor and El Gallo were the good guys in this particular story. Curious children hovered around the bodies, and three men were already arguing over the guns that had fallen to the ground. Héctor left to join El Gallo.

"I killed him, didn't I?"

"If you hadn't shot him, he would have gotten me. I guess I owe you one, pal."

"I killed him, didn't I?" repeated El Gallo.

"Yeah, you killed him, and I killed the other one. And it feels like shit, I know, even when it's in self-defense."

El Gallo put the Colt back in his jacket pocket and started walking. Héctor followed him. The crowd parted to let them pass.

"They shot first, *jefe*. We all saw it," said a gap-toothed paperboy.

El Gallo turned to Héctor and asked, "Where to now?"

"Away from here. I need time to think. And I don't want to have to deal with the cops."

They walked side by side and the circle of onlookers closed again behind them.

"Where'd you get the gun?" asked Héctor.

"I've had it in the office for a while now, since that time a couple of years ago when they tried to kill you. And when Carlos said that these two had been hanging around, I thought...I never thought it would really happen. I've never even fired a shot before in my life, and then I go and hit this guy the first time. He was moving and everything. I only wanted to scare him off."

They turned the corner and, absurdly, no one stopped them, no one followed them. Héctor glanced over his shoulder now and then, but the city remained the same. They turned onto Reforma at the statue of Carlos the Fifth, and there they could hear the first sirens.

"Don't worry about it, Gallo. Those two were hired killers, they got what was coming to them. We don't owe them anything."

"I killed him," said El Gallo.

The sun was climbing higher now, lighting up the brilliant morning, as Héctor Belascoarán Shayne and El Gallo Villareal went their separate ways.

He desperately needed someplace to think and, following his rule of keeping to the most unlikely places, he ended up at a carnival near Buenavista station.

He wandered past the rickety rides, big pieces of metal rising and falling and spinning around with an endless screeching. The merry-go-round music seemed unusually subdued. He assiduously avoided the shooting gallery, and headed over to the Ferris wheel, where, with fifty pesos of encouragement, he was able to convince the operator to start it up and give him a solo ride.

A solitary traveler, Héctor Belascoarán Shayne saw again and again in his mind the double impact that had felled the black-haired man in the gray suit. He saw again the look of release on the dead men's faces. He cursed this whole weird story that had been forced upon him, that had filled his hands with corpses, confusion, and blood. At its highest point, the Ferris wheel gave the detective a view of the rooftops of the Colonia Santa María, the Nonoalco Towers, the overpass on Insurgentes, the railyard behind the station, the furniture stores on San Cosme, and the buildings that housed the headquarters of the ruling Institutional Revolutionary Party. Aiming at the PRI building, he hocked a gob of spit and watched it trace a lovely curve down onto the roof of a dart booth.

He was thirty-three years old and he'd wasted the first thirty years of his life, or, to put it another way, the first thirty had wasted themselves on him. To change your job, your patterns, your style, your ideas, the familiar places, to go in search of something, scratching like a leper at the skin of your own country, to try and find a place, trying to adapt to the encircling violence; it all sounded good, and he'd lived through it and even enjoyed himself in the process. In three years he hadn't lost his sense of humor, his ability to laugh at himself. And he'd learned to accept the chaos at face value, the uneasiness, the fear, the surprise. He had plenty of easy truths, empty platitudes. What he didn't have was the slightest idea of why they were after him, who they were or where they were from. He was beset by the forces of evil. The lousy stinking faceless fucked-up forces of evil. He laughed at himself for needing to give a name, even such a ridiculous one, to his unknown aggressors. Maybe that was enough. That smile. He was going to find the forces of evil and kick their butts. The assholes who'd sent him dead Romans, photographs, and subway cops moonlighting as hired killers. He needed to get it all out on the table, put it all into some kind of order, feel out the angles, and get down to work. Fast. Get the whole thing moving so fast that it would spin out of their control, force them to make a mistake, show themselves, show their hand, and finally let him into the game. And then, bam, he was going to take them for all they were worth. The man he killed today was dead and there was no bringing him back, and if there were going to be more dead men, then so be it. And if they killed him, for whatever reason, in whatever way, then he was going to die. Better to die than to eat shit.

Oblivious to the detective's euphoric mood, the Ferris wheel kept turning stubbornly around and around, even after Belascoarán wished that it would stop so he could get off and go find a place to write some notes and put his thoughts in order.

The machine finally ground to a halt with Héctor at the highest point, and he realized the most important thing of all: if this was about good versus evil, he was going to be the good guy. One-eyed and limping, but the good guy in the end.

But the two dead men still stared endlessly skyward, past the shoulder of the detective who looked down at them from above, ready to deliver the coup de grace.

The rabbit was waiting for him. It sat in the middle of the rug, watching the door with shiny red eyes. Around it, dozens of tiny black dots. It hopped across the carpet and licked Héctor's shoe. It had eaten part of a chair seat and most of the broom. Fortunately it hadn't tried to eat any books.

Héctor picked it up and went into the kitchen, summarizing out loud, for the rabbit's benefit, his theories on the forces of evil and how to kick their butts. He filled a dish with water and got out a couple of carrots. Then he took off his jacket and his shirt. Just in case, he stuck his revolver into the waistband of his pants. He took the Gerry Mulligan record off the stereo and put on Louis Armstrong, then he sat down at the table with his notebook and two bottles of soda pop.

1. They send me two corpses (one in the flesh, the other a picture).

They want to scare me, not frame me, because they remove the corpse. To make their point, ticket to New York.

Apparently they want me to stop doing something that has something to do with the dead men. But they're wrong, since I wasn't doing anything.

2. The dead men worked for Zorak, a magician-contortionist-escape artist-daredevil-showman who died in 1973 when he fell out of a helicopter.

The third man in this group, Captain Freshie, knows me by sight and ran away when he saw me.

3. "Them," the forces of evil, are highly organized: ticket to New York, removal of body, subway cops, etc.

At that moment the doorbell rang.

Héctor took out his gun and stepped to one side of the door.

"Who is it?" he asked, placing his back to the wall and raising his gun.

"Marino Saiz, at your service...If I could have just a moment of your time..."

Héctor opened the door. There was something about the voice that reassured him.

A small, neatly dressed man entered the apartment, gripping a large sample case in each hand.

Héctor tucked his gun into the back of his waistband and crossed his arms, waiting.

The man put his cases on the floor, briefly contemplated the shirtless detective and, with a resigned expression (it was getting harder all the time to find decent clients), he launched into his sales pitch.

"I've come to offer you the best and most complete collection of *zarzuelas* available on record today..."

Héctor smiled. The man took it as a sign of encouragement and forged ahead: "This rare collection consists of eight long-playing records with a veritable treasure trove of classical *zarzuelas*, the very same folk songs that have moved Spanish monarchs to tears and sweetened half a century of Iberian life..."

Héctor's smile broadened. The man sensed victory and continued: "And, if you buy now, I am empowered to give to you free, absolutely free, an entire bonus album of today's hottest disco hits, along with a personally autographed photograph of John Travolta."

"Where'd you get the autographed picture of John Travolta?" asked the detective.

"They come already signed, all I do is write your name at the top, with a dedication, whatever you want it to say. With the same handwriting and everything. I haven't been in this business for eleven years for nothing."

"What was that bit about the Spanish monarchy?" asked Héctor.

"Listen, I couldn't give two farts in hell for the Spanish monarchy. I'm a Socialist. But the *zarzuela*, now there's a thing of real beauty. As a matter of fact, this collection includes—"

"Don't say another word. You've made your sale," said the detective.

Héctor had him sign the photograph, "To Gilberto Gómez Letras, from his good friend, John Travolta." The whole thing cost him 645 pesos. When the door shut behind the little man, it occurred to Héctor that he'd never heard a *zarzuela* in his life.

He ate in a grimy café around the corner from his apartment. When he was finished, he wiped the last bits of rice pudding from his lips, took a wrinkled piece of paper from his pocket, and went over the list:

1. Señorita S

2. Captain Freshie

3. Subway police?

4. Death of Zorak, details?

He folded the paper and put it back in his pocket. The afternoon sported a big, warm sun that filled the windows and the sky with orange-tinged rays of light.

He had a plan, he was hungry for a fight, and he had his loaded .45. He was ready to go after them.

He bought the afternoon papers on Insurgentes. On page three he found a story with the first reports of the morning's gun battle. Judicial Police Commander Silva (that name again, what was the connection?), who has been placed in charge of the investigation, would comment only that the two men killed in this morning's exchange were members of the subway police force, and that they had been gunned down by a single shooter (they'd left El Gallo out of it). Not one of the hundreds of eyewitnesses has come forward with a description of the unknown gunman.

The story failed to mention that the two subway cops had fired first. It concluded with some speculation about revenge killings, and the settling of accounts among drug dealers.

He walked as he read, banging his head first against a low tree branch, then a ladder sticking out the back of a telephone repair truck. Insurgentes was heavy with traffic. Passengers hung like bunches of fruit from passing buses. Everywhere cars braked loudly and clouds of dust mingled with thick exhaust. Noise, everywhere noise. He walked hurriedly along the avenue, and turned right onto San Luis Potosí. Were they following him? He took the next right, then ducked into a building that housed the offices of a construction company. He kept his back to the street and watched the passersby reflected in the glass that covered the tenant directory. After a couple of minutes, he gave up and went back out, walking briskly, half running. Back when he was married, his wife had tired of complaining to Héctor about the way he walked: he was impossible to keep up with, he never wanted to stop and window-shop, he took everything in on the fly, always with that same short, quick step. Now he looked alternately at the ground and up at the sky, driven to experience as much of the afternoon as possible before it faded into evening.

Finally, he found the building he was looking for and went up to the fifth floor, to the offices of a talent agency where they owed him a favor. He went in, headed straight for the assistant director's office, and without knocking or checking with the secretary, went in.

"Hello, detective."

"How're you doing, Yolanda?"

The woman held one telephone in her left hand and balanced another one on her right shoulder. She made a gesture for him to wait, and continued her conversation.

Héctor looked around the walls, the newspaper clippings, photographs, and diplomas.

Yolanda hung up both telephones at once.

"What can I do for you?"

Detective, reporter, and prostitute; they were perhaps the only jobs that required keeping a list of hundreds of pseud-ofriends and superficial acquaintances.

"I need to find the wife of a guy who used to call himself Zorak. She used the stage name of Señorita S, or something like that…"

"Zorak, the daredevil, the one who fell out of the helicopter?"

"You win the prize."

"That's a tough one. She's not in the business anymore, as far as I know. What does she do?"

"From what I can tell, she worked as a model before she hooked up with Zorak. I hear she—"

"Wait a minute! A cross-eyed girl?"

"Yeah, I think so. I've never actually seen her."

"Márgara Duran! Now I remember. She does some modeling for an agency in the Zona Rosa."

Yolanda opened a drawer and took out a bottle of cognac.

"Care for a drink, detective?"

She was about forty, very striking, blonde, lots of makeup, full of energy and good cheer. Two years ago her lover had tried to throw acid into her face and Héctor had intervened, breaking two of the guy's ribs with a heavy brass ashtray. It had all happened in the middle of another case, completely unconnected.

"No thanks. Alcohol kills."

"So does sobriety."

"Details, Yolanda, details. Do you know anything about a stripper named Melina, who works in a club called La Fuente de Venus, on San Juan de Letran?"

"I've never heard of the club. I've heard a little about Melina, though. She's from Ciudad Juárez, a nobody, a stripper and a showgirl. Used to go out with some politician or other."

"So what else is new?" said Héctor, and he stood up to go.

His brother, Carlos, lay on the floor, reading. Marina opened the door for him. She had a couple of pieces from a jigsaw puzzle in her hand, and, after greeting the detective with a kiss, she went back to the table to fit one of them in place. The tiny rooftop apartment was packed, that was the only word he could think to describe it: books everywhere, a table, four chairs squeezed between table and walls, a kitchen the size of a closet, barely big enough to hold a stove and a refrigerator.

He stepped across to the table, with its nearly completed jigsaw puzzle of a Paul Klee painting.

"How's it going, brother?" asked Carlos from the floor. Héctor shrugged.

"Do you have a phone book?" he asked.

"How about a soda to go with it?" said Marina, leaving her puzzle to pull the phone book out from underneath one of the chairs, and crossing over into the kitchen.

The telephone was on the table. Héctor dialed.

"Mendiola please...Hey, you never told me the other day all the details about how Zorak died. His name keeps turning up all over the place...Can you put some clips together for me? I'd appreciate it...I'll be by tomorrow morning. Thanks, buddy."

Héctor hung up. Marina was looking at him.

"Carlos, wasn't Zorak that guy who fell out of the helicopter four or five years ago?"

"Six," said Héctor.

"The one everybody said trained the Halcones," said Carlos, sitting up.

"The Halcones?" asked Héctor.

"Where have you been living all these years?" asked Carlos.

"Right here, in Mexico," answered the detective.

Marina handed him a bottle of orange soda.

Chapter VIII

The Halcones

If anyone is suspect in this country, it's the police.
—*Luis González de Alba*

This shadowy, violent organization had shown evidence of its existence before. The first time was during the Ayotla Textile strike, when a paramilitary group appeared out of nowhere, shooting and beating the picketers before the laughing gaze of the police. Later on there were hints of what was to come during the demonstrations at the Politécnico leading up to the tenth of June, 1970. But to the innocent eye of the student left, these warning signs appeared as nothing more than a further indication of the continued growth of the right-wing student gangs in the dreary days since the debacle of 1968. None of it seemed to go much beyond the small gangs that then held sway on campus, dealing drugs and financed by the university administration itself. Gangs of eight, ten, fifteen lowlifes who would get drunk and run wild, mugging, raping, hazing—and then justified their existence by doubling as a glee club during football games. So when the decision was made to take to the streets again on the tenth of June, nobody expected to have to face more than the standard, sullen-eyed riot police, the dark blue stain, bolstered now by the purchase of six new Molotov cocktail-proof armored vehicles, to which campus mythology attributed any number of extraordinary powers and advanced weaponry: tear gas, rubber bullets, machine guns, water hoses, deafening sirens, infrared night vision, plus, in a more exotic vein, the ability to spray paint, play the national anthem, and even fart, not to mention the obvious capacity to run down anybody stupid enough to get in their way.

And sure enough, there they were, painted a dull grayish blue, taking up positions around the Politécnico campus at the Casco de Santo Tomás. And backed by two battalions of riot police, revitalized over the last three years (after the massive desertions of '68) with new recruits from the countryside: landless peasants from Puebla, Tlaxcala, Oaxaca, who had survived the brutality of training camp and were just beginning to enjoy the petty powers, the impunity, conferred on them by their uniform. They'd been indoctrinated to see themselves as the last bulwark of the fatherland, arrayed against the godless, communistic students, who, so they were told, hated the Virgin of Guadalupe and sought to destroy Mexico itself. They hid their fear behind our own.

But they were only there to scare us, really. Anyone who pisses his pants over a couple of thousand riot police hasn't lived. If they were really going to clamp down, they wouldn't be so obvious about it. So we marched right past them, looking them in the eye, accepting the challenge, staring down the prodigious technicians of evil.

There was a rumor going around that if you jammed a potato up the exhaust pipe of one of the new antiriot vehicles it would blow up like a squashed toad. We tried to guess the diameter of the exhaust pipes as we walked by, and to estimate the required density of the potato, which we'd forgotten to bring anyway, because who really believed…

We marched along Melchor Ocampo, San Cosme, Avenida de los Gallos. Watch out ahead, there's a break in the line to the west, at the iron fence that runs around the Teachers College and the Politécnico, but all the same we started to file into the esplanade of the Casco de Santo Tomás, where our new demands were to be announced: hands off the University of Nuevo León; union democracy; freedom for political prisoners. We had all come to more or less the same conclusions by then, that the government needed to consolidate the present opening, that it couldn't afford a new wave of repression, and that the public statements of President Echevarría were practically an invitation to take to the streets. It was a chance for us to recuperate some of the power we'd lost, and an opportunity for him to demonstrate clearly that the barbaric Mexico of his predecessor, Díaz Ordaz, no longer existed, that the center could be widened to include more of the fringe. So there we were, all decked out in blue jeans and red, blue, tan shirts, corduroy trousers, bandanas around our necks, khaki jackets despite the heat, and the girls in their brightly colored pants, and the white dress shirts of the students from the provinces, who finally had their chance now, having been too young for the Movement in '68 (the Movement with a capital M, the starting point, the line drawn in the sand of our lives, our point of reference as human beings in this country, in this life).

Surprisingly, even with the heavy police presence, ten thousand people turned out to demonstrate. More, maybe as many as fifteen thousand, and we took our collective fear and we turned it around to show that fear couldn't stop us. And then out came the red banners, carefully at first, out from the jackets under which they'd been lovingly concealed, unfurled now, and other banners too, with the familiar slogans under new acronyms. It was pure euphoria, a euphoria tinged by the bittersweet taste of a fear defeated but still close by.

There was barely time to greet friends, identify organizations, recognize faces. Ah, how the palms slapped, the hands gripped, with the thumb pointing at the other's heart, the fingers closing, the feel of your friend's rough skin. The Econ students from the National University led off the march, followed by the Politécnico's own School of Economics, complete with the familiar faces of students recently released from prison or returned from exile. The march followed the Avenida de los Gallos, then turned along Avenida de los

Maestros, with the first songs ringing through the air. By the time the last marchers had left the Casco, the head of the line had already reached the Calzada México-Tacuba.

That was when it happened. They came out of side streets, shouting "*Viva Che Guevara!*" The riot police opened spaces for them to pass, and then their picket signs turned into clubs, and they attacked the crowd. The "*Viva Che Guevara*" became a surprising "*Viva el presidente, cabrones!*" They came in through Sor Juana, Amado Nervo, Alzate. At one spot they clashed head on with a group of teenagers from the Preparatoria Popular, who recovered from the initial surprise, regrouped, and fought back, while the police held up the march at the front of the line. There was hand-to-hand fighting in the street, people were running everywhere, the line of marchers was broken.

Then the first shots were heard. The riot police had pulled back, the marchers had started to move again toward the Cosmos Cinema, and it seemed as though the intruders had been defeated. There were only about three hundred of them, after all, even if they did carry clubs and knew kendo and shouted at the top of their lungs when they charged, and seemed to be well trained and organized. Even with all that, they were no match for the purely Mexican joy, the *alegría*, of an entire generation of students who, despite their university education, had grown up in the streets, had known the day-to-day struggle of survival, and had been brought together in the movement of '68. That's when the first shots could be heard, a burst of machine-gun fire over the heads of the marchers, fired from a passing car, and then they returned in force, armed with M1 rifles, and pistols, and automatic weapons, and more clubs, and the police opened up again to let them pass.

And some of us, those who could still hear, those who were listening, heard the attackers' strange war cry: *Halcones!* Falcons! *Halcones!*

The afternoon ended in terror, more than forty people killed, Red Cross workers attacked when they tried to carry away the wounded, the Halcones shooting blindly into the crowd, the police cordon, followed by the arrival of the army, massive arrests, house-to-house searches, the line of marchers shattered, the rooftop chases, random sniper fire that lasted until dark, the impassive riot police, watching, occasionally lobbing a few tear gas canisters at stray groups of demonstrators who couldn't quite bring themselves to flee the horror and stayed on to roam aimlessly through the streets as though they had a debt of honor that impelled them to remain as witnesses to the massacre.

Around seven-thirty it started to rain, and the puddles of blood were washed from the sidewalks. The fence around the Teachers College had been pulled down under the weight of students climbing over it to escape. An ambulance with its tires shot out sat abandoned at the intersection of México-Tacuba and Avenida de los Maestros, the red light still spinning around on top as the last few shots echoed in the twilight. By eight o'clock, the army had established control and tanks rolled down the abandoned streets.

The official explanation wrote the whole thing off as an unfortunate clash between antagonistic student groups. But then there were the photographs of the army-issue M1 rifles, and the riot police allowing the armed men to pass unopposed, and the tape recordings from the police radio frequency, over which police officers directed the Halcones' attack. And the discovery by Guillermo Jordan, a reporter for *Ultimas Noticias*, of the trucks in which the Halcones had been transported, property of the Mexico City government, the city emblem carefully painted over in gray. And the training camps near the airport and in the Colonia Aragon, and the recruitment of the Halcones from within the army, and the involvement of high-ranking army and police officers in their training. But the dead remained dead, despite all the scandal and the outrage…And no one was ever brought to trial, and when an investigation was finally called for, eight years later, all the records had disappeared.

Chapter IX

One breathes easier in the middle of the storm.
—*Mikhail Bakunin*

It was around three in the morning when Héctor, stifling a yawn, turned the ignition key in the VW. The stripper emerged from the Fuente de Venus, her hips swinging, a fire red scarf wrapped around her head. A waiter accompanied her to a Mustang parked on the street.

The woman drove slowly, and Héctor had no problem following in the car he'd borrowed from his sister. They went straight down Reforma to the Ángel, where the woman left the avenue, drove for a few more minutes, then parked on one of the side streets of the Colonia Cuauhtémoc. A few minutes later, the lights went on in a third-floor apartment. Héctor drove past the building, turned his car around, and parked in a spot where he could keep an eye on the front door. He thought it over, then lit a cigarette and settled down to wait. He preferred to wait now and act later, in the light of day. The woman could lead him to Captain Freshie; the question was how to go about it. He stretched out as best he could and prepared to wait out the rest of the night.

He catnapped restlessly, an unhappy, superficial sleep, his muscles cramped, little birds filling his head. At six in the morning a Red Cross ambulance raced by at top speed and the city seemed to come back to life: a school bus, a paper vendor on a bicycle, three or four maids walking to work.

He crawled out of the car, trying unsuccessfully to locate the source of the diffuse pain in his back. He decided to grab a bite to eat before beginning his interrogation of Miss Melina, with tango soundtrack. He had taken only a few steps away from the car, in the opposite direction from the showgirl's apartment, when he instinctively turned his head. A red car had pulled up in front of the building. Two men got out. It was the same thing all over again, dark glasses, cheap blue and gray suits. He walked halfway down the block and hid behind a newspaper kiosk. The two men exchanged a few words with the driver of their car, who remained behind the wheel, and entered the building.

There they were, the forces of evil.

Héctor put his hand on his gun, caressed the butt.

He had to think fast. It was getting lighter, and more and more cars could be seen passing at the corner on Reforma. A shiver went through him. To wait or to act? Maybe he was just paranoid. He was paralyzed by doubt. If the two men who had gone inside came out while he was taking care of the driver, he'd be screwed. If he waited…

He walked toward the waiting car, trying to keep out of the line of sight of the rear-view mirror. The street was empty. He took out his gun. The driver was picking his nose when Héctor pushed the barrel of the gun up against his temple.

"Hands on the wheel, pal."

"You sure you know how to work that thing?"

"When I pull the trigger, lead comes out. Pretty nifty."

Slowly, the man brought his hands to the wheel, but before he could finish, Héctor hit him as hard as he could with the gun barrel across the temple. The man let out a sigh and collapsed across the steering wheel. Héctor opened the door and pushed. The guy's ass pointed out at the street. Héctor pushed again. There was blood on the seat. Maybe I went too far, Héctor thought. Maybe the guy doesn't have anything to do with the forces of evil after all. He laughed. The forces of evil. It sounded too grandiose for this stupid, blood-smeared monkey. Keeping an eye on the door to Melina's building, he got into the car and turned the key, then drove toward

Reforma. He stopped at the corner and searched the motionless heap next to him. A few drops of blood oozed from the man's temple. A .38 revolver, a subway police ID card in the name of Augustín Porfirio Olvera, a small stack of porno pictures held together with a rubber band, some money. He dumped it all onto the seat, drove around the block, and parked in front of an empty lot. He pocketed the man's gun and ID and walked quickly back to his own car. Nothing. The street was as empty as before. It would be a good place to stage a duel. The set for an urban Western. An empty street in the Colonia Cuauhtémoc at seven-thirty in the morning. What came next?

He crossed over to the apartment building and started up the stairs. There were two apartments on the third floor. Number 302 was the one facing the street where the light had shone the night before. The door was closed. Did the building have an inner patio? Could he get to the apartment from the roof? He continued upstairs. The third floor was the last one, and the staircase ended at a gray door. He went out onto the roof and crossed to the central airshaft, looking down on the windows of number 302: the bathroom window, and another one covered with a red curtain. It was at least twelve feet from the roof down to the bathroom window. Maybe it would be easier to get in from the patio, using the ladder that leaned against one corner. The patio was empty. But he could only get to it through one of the ground-floor apartments. He started down again. As he went past number 302, the door opened, and Héctor found himself face-to-face with a man about thirty-five years old, with very dark, straight hair, a thin mustache over thick lips, dressed in a suit, his necktie loose and crooked under the collar of a white shirt. That's all he had time to notice. The man's left hand went to the gun at his waist. Héctor pushed past him, pulling his gun from his shoulder holster as he ran headlong down the stairs. The first shot exploded from behind him and chunks of plaster flew from the wall over his head. At the landing, Héctor turned, raised his gun, waited for the man to cross his line of sight, and squeezed the trigger. The sound of the shot and the smell of cordite filled the stairway. The man tumbled, raising his hands to his throat, and landed facedown at Héctor's feet. One down, one to go. He picked up the dead man, shielding himself behind the body while he kept his gun pointed up the vacant stairway. The dead man was heavy, and slippery with blood. A pair of shots rang out as the other man fired from the doorway at his partner's corpse. Héctor felt the impact as a bullet smashed into the dead man's chest. He dropped the body and aimed at the shooter as he was turning to duck back inside. He shot twice. One bullet caught the man in the shoulder and spun him around, the other one hit him in the base of the skull, exploding his head like a rotten melon.

Héctor only had a few seconds to work. The stripper sat in her living room, perched on the edge of an orange armchair, staring at the ceiling, strangely immobile. A thin line of blood ran down from bruised lips. But she was alive. A few yards away, Captain Freshie had gone on to join his old friends Leobardo the Roman and Don Agustín, the owner of the Fuente de Venus. He lay in a heap on the rug with his throat slashed. Héctor tried to get the woman to stand up. She was deadweight. Her glassy eyes stared out at nothing. He dropped her arm and ran down the stairs, without taking another look at the dead men sprawled in the hallway.

When he got to the street he slowed to a walk and looked up at the apartment building as though he were a casual passerby. A few windows opened up, and a woman in a bathrobe appeared in the door of a neighboring building.

"Did you hear shots?"

Héctor had his back to her, and he didn't want to turn around where she would see the blood on his shirt, only partly covered by his jacket.

"I think so. Better be careful, you never know around here."

By the time he turned the corner, his heart was jumping like a maddened acrobat. He had trouble drawing breath, and he felt a pain in his chest. He turned up his jacket collar, buried his hands in his pockets. He felt cold, a terrible cold. He'd killed two more men.

The blood had dried on his shirt, and the cold feeling was replaced by a sharp, very intense headache. Half an hour later he went over it all in his head and realized that they'd almost killed him twice. If the first man had only aimed a little lower as he was running down the stairs, if the other one had aimed for his head instead of at his dead partner's torso. Two chances. Two misses. He drove the red car around again—what was it, eight or nine times now?—along the oval street that circumnavigated the Parque México. He'd transferred the unconscious driver to the trunk in a parking lot in the Zona Rosa. Now he needed to figure out his next move. If this were a mystery novel, it would have all become clear to him; even when the detective was uncertain, at least his uncertainty was always clear. It was nothing like this. His hands still shook, and at regular intervals he would break out in a cold sweat. He smiled at the rear-view mirror. Is that how another man's death felt? Was that it?

He had to feel hate. His fear and his sad smile weren't going to be enough to keep his hunters from killing him. He'd been lucky so far. But that wouldn't last forever. He had to hate. And there were things he had to know. He pointed the car toward his house in the Colonia Roma.

Merlín, the semiretired electrician who was also his landlord, stood out in front of his building when Héctor pulled up.

"Detective. It's a damn good thing you weren't at home last night."

"What's up, Merlín?"

"There were two or three unsavory characters nosing around here last night. I caught them waiting for you on the landing. I didn't like their looks. They finally left around six this morning."

"Will you do me a favor?"

"Whatever you want, friend. And if the State's the enemy, then so much the better."

"I don't know if it's the State, or just a piece of the State. The problem is I've got this son of a bitch unconscious here in the trunk. Will you keep an eye on him, while I run upstairs? I don't want him to get away."

"Let me get a hammer and I'll be right back."

The electrician disappeared into his street-front repair shop and came out a moment later armed with a hammer. They came looking for me here before they went to the stripper's place, thought Héctor. He got out of the car and took the steps two at a time.

The door to his apartment had been forced, and he pushed it open with two fingers. The rabbit lay dead in the middle of the rug. They'd cut its throat.

Héctor went into his bedroom and grabbed two clean pairs of socks, a shirt, and switched his brown jacket for a black one with bigger pockets, into which he threw two clips for his .45 automatic. He loaded a fresh clip into the gun. As he turned to go, he picked up the book he'd been reading and shoved it into another pocket. He closed the door softly and said a mental good-bye to the rabbit.

Merlín kept watch out front, sitting on the trunk of the car.

"Merlín, I have to ask you to bury my rabbit for me."

"What rabbit?"

"The one that's lying dead on my living room rug."

"A rabbit rabbit?"

"That's right."

"Whatever you say."

"I might not be back for a few days…If I don't come back, I want you to have my books on the Spanish Civil War. They're on the bookshelf in the hallway. I inherited them from my father."

"I hope it doesn't come to that," the old man said, smiling, and waving good-bye with the hammer.

He parked the car in the woods, at a place where the pine trees thinned out a bit. He took out his automatic. The sun filtered through the treetops, glinting first off the driver's-side mirror, then off the bluish metal of the gun. The distant hum of cars on the highway mixed with the trill of a few birds and the soft whistle of wind in the branches. He unlocked the trunk and the lid swung up by itself, squeaking. The hunched form inside appeared to be dead. Héctor took a step back, aimed the gun, and waited. There was no movement.

"I'll count to ten, then I start shooting."

The man lay motionless, hunched over, a spot of dry blood at his temple, his mouth open.

"One…two…three…four…five…six…"

"Wait. Just give me a second. I feel like crap."

He raised himself slowly, supporting his weight on the lip of the trunk.

"My dear Porfirio, you're in a whole lot of deep shit," said the detective.

The man stared at him. There was fear in his eyes, but in his mouth, in the hard set of his jaw, there was only the desire to kill.

"First of all, your two friends are dead. I don't care if I have to kill four or five of you people. You ought to know that by now. One more, it's all the same to me. If you tell me what I want to know, I'll probably let you go. I don't get any thrill out of killing anyone…So you tell me. Are you going to cooperate or do I shoot you?"

The man looked at Héctor's eyes, then at his gun, and back at his eyes.

"You can only see out of one eye."

"I lost the other one in the war. But I'm a better shot this way. I don't have to close my eye when I aim. It's already closed, so to speak," answered Héctor.

He was going to have to kill him if he wouldn't talk. He didn't give a damn about Agustín Porfirio Olvera. That's one thing he'd learned over the last two days, that the lives of gunmen working for the forces of evil didn't mean a thing to him. They might die ugly, with too much blood, but they weren't worth crying over.

"Where do you work?"

"You already know. I'm a cop on the subway."

"Who's your immediate superior?"

"Commander Sánchez."

"Are you part of the regular city police, or are you separate?"

"Separate. We get our papers through the city, but we work for the subway and the subway pays us."

"How long have you worked there?"

"Since 1971."

"Where're you from?"

He looked at the detective for several seconds. For the first time he didn't answer right away, as though the question took him by surprise.

"I was born in Pachuca, but we moved to Mexico City when I was a kid."

"How old are you?"

"Twenty-nine."

"Married?"

He nodded.

"How many old ladies have you got?"

The man turned his head to the side and started to smile, but he caught himself, and instead brought his hand to the cut on his temple, hoping to win Héctor's sympathy.

"There used to be this bunch of thugs that worked for the city, they'd drive around in pickup trucks without plates and hassle sidewalk vendors, throw their stuff on the ground, wreck their stands, steal stuff. You worked with them, didn't you?"

"How'd you know?"

"Just a hunch."

He looked older than twenty-nine, hardened, his narrow eyes rimmed with bags, his hair greasy.

"How much do you make?"

"Nine grand a month, plus bonuses."

"What kind of bonuses?"

"For punctuality. And for special jobs."

"Like what?"

"Like killing you."

"How much were you supposed to get for that?"

"Twenty grand."

"Apiece?"

"Between the three of us."

"Who was paying?"

He didn't answer. Héctor raised his gun and pointed, first at his chest, then at his left arm. If he didn't soften him up now, he wouldn't get any more out of him.

"I'm going to shoot you in the arm to start with. If I can't soften you up now, I never will, and then I won't find out what I need to know. If I shoot you in the arm, then the leg, and then if I shoot your toes off, pretty soon you'll be counting the hairs in your boss's asshole for me. Here goes…"

"Captain Estrella."

"Commander Sánchez doesn't have anything to do with it?"

"Sánchez is new. He's not one of us."

"Who's us?"

"We all went in together in '71."

"When? Late summer?"

"Yeah, around then."

"After the tenth of June."

"Right."

"When did they send you out to kill me?"

"Yesterday afternoon."

"Did you know the ones who got killed over on Bucareli?"

He nodded.

Héctor jumped from question to question without taking time to consider the answers, picking at him here and there, fishing for bits of information, trying to be random enough to keep the man off guard and telling the truth.

"How many of you got jobs as subway cops?"

"Thirty or forty."

"And the rest?"

"Some of them got work as bodyguards, some of them went into the army, some of them went freelance, some of them went home. Some of them are dead."

"Who's behind Captain Estrella?"

"Beats me."

"Did you train with Zorak?"

"Sure. He was a good guy. Everybody liked him."

"Who killed Captain Freshie?"

"Must have been the Chink, the one who was with me this morning."

"Did you know Captain Freshie?"

"He was one of Zorak's guys."

"What kind of training did Zorak give you?"

"Just physical fitness stuff. Exercises, martial arts."

"Who killed Zorak?"

"Beats me."

"Who killed Zorak's other two friends, the Roman and the other guy?"

"The Chink. He was always good with a knife...Did you really kill him?"

Héctor nodded. He was getting tired. It almost seemed as though death couldn't touch either of them, as if they wore their dead men on their chests like devout Catholics wear religious medallions. Just to demonstrate their faith.

"Do you have an office somewhere?"

"Who?"

"The subway police."

"Yes."

"Where?"

"In the Juanacatlán station. We report to Commander Sánchez in the morning and he tells us what we're supposed to do."

"What about Captain Estrella?"

"Him and Barrios, they give us the other jobs, the under-the-table stuff."

"Does Sánchez know?"

"He ought to. He's not that dumb."

"Who got you the subway jobs?"

"Beats me. All they said was to show up at such and such a place on such and such a day, with a couple of photographs and this letter we're going to give you, and that was it..."

"Did you carry a gun on the tenth of June?"

"Yes."

"A rifle?"

"No, a pistol."

"How many people did you shoot?"

"I only fired in the air."

"When they told you to come after me, what did they say exactly?"

"They said that you'd killed Guzmán and the Panther and that you knew too much, that you could bring the whole thing about the tenth of June out into the open again."

If he shot him in the leg to immobilize him, he'd bleed to death before anyone found him there in the middle of the Desierto de los Leones. If he let him go, he'd go tell his people things that Héctor didn't want them to know just yet.

"Take off your clothes, Agustín Porfirio," instructed the detective, pointing the gun at his head. "I'm going to do you a favor…Don't worry, I won't get you pregnant."

"Go ahead and kill me, just don't make fun of me," said the man, as he loosened his wrinkled gray necktie.

❉ ❉ ❉

Mendiola was out, but he'd left a manila envelope on his desk for the detective. Héctor tore the envelope open and sat down to read in the middle of the busy newsroom. Two sports photographers walked by, and a few desks away the entertainment editor flirted with someone on the telephone in a voice much louder than necessary.

The clippings in the envelopes told a simple story: Zorak had been hired by the developers of a new housing subdivision to appear during a special weekend promotion. Zorak was to perform various daredevil stunts and acts of magic, beginning with his arrival by helicopter. He would lower himself from the helicopter by a long cable attached to his wrist, then release the cable thirty feet above the ground and drop onto a pile of sand. The show had been advertised in the newspapers and sound cars had been announcing it for a week in the surrounding neighborhoods; there was a large turnout.

Around noon the helicopter flew into sight. Zorak lowered himself down on the cable but, about five hundred yards from the appointed spot, the helicopter rose violently upward and the cable snapped. Zorak fell at least two hundred feet onto one of the subdivision's newly paved streets. He was dead by the time the Red Cross paramedics, on hand to treat the occasional case of heat shock, got to him. His wrist was badly abraded.

That was all. The clippings reported that the helicopter had hit an updraft, and the safety mechanism that connected Zorak's wrist to the cable had broken under the sudden stress.

Héctor replaced the clippings in the envelope and scribbled a note of thanks to Mendiola.

He'd left the subway cop tied naked to a tree in the Desierto de los Leones. Now he had to ditch the red car and retrieve his sister's VW. He called Elisa from a phone booth outside the newspaper and told her where to find her car, and what to say if the police should question her.

He gave her enough time to get to the Colonia Cuauhtémoc, then parked the red car a couple of blocks from the showgirl's apartment and walked over to Reforma. From there he could see the door to the building and the VW parked where he'd left it. There was a squad car parked in front of the building, but the street itself was quiet and free of onlookers. It had probably been several hours already since they'd carted away the dead men. Elisa arrived in a taxi and got into her car without anyone stopping her. She pulled away from the curb, picked Héctor up at the corner, and he directed her to where he'd left the red car.

"I want you to follow me."

"What's going on?"

"I'm going to set off some fireworks at the Juanacatlán subway station. Follow me. You'll see."

"You get me involved in the weirdest shit, Héctor."

They drove in their separate cars for ten minutes. Héctor turned on the radio and tried to locate the twelve o'clock news on Radio 1000. He couldn't get it to come in, and settled instead for a tropical music station, where the great Acerina and his amazing horns laid down some licks that would have turned the National Symphony green with envy.

He left the Circuito Interior and pulled into a gas station, where he bought a gallon of gasoline in a plastic jug.

He drove for another minute and then stopped the red car on Pedro Antonio de los Santos, directly in front of the Juanacatlán station. He splashed the gasoline all over the car's interior. Elisa waited in the VW a hundred yards farther on. Héctor got out of the car, took a piece of rope left over from the trussing of the subway cop, soaked it in gasoline, and stuck one end into the car's gas tank. It made a perfect fuse. This done, Héctor lit a cigarette, then touched his lighter to the end of the rope. He barely had time to run ten feet. The flame leaped the length of the gassoaked rope, and two seconds later the street was rocked by the explosion, the car consumed in a tremendous fireball. Héctor was thrown forward by a burst of superheated air filled with bits of burning debris. He raced down the block and jumped into his sister's car.

"You're such an extremist, Héctor. What'd you do, soak the whole thing in gasoline?"

"I don't want to hear it. I almost blew myself up. Can we get out of here?"

Behind them, the burning car was drawing a crowd in front of the station entrance. Elisa pulled into the street.

"What'd you do that for?"

"To let them know that this is for real."

"That what's for real?"

"The war between the association of independent detectives and the forces of evil."

"What's the association of independent detectives?"

"Me. I've had to kill three men in the last two days."

Elisa looked at him without speaking. Héctor stretched out in the car seat and let his head fall back.

"Let's get something to eat," he said.

They let him walk right into the studio, no questions asked. It seemed to be common practice to let clients, or those appearing to be clients, into the studio while a shoot was in progress. It was just another aspect of the place's self-conscious air of sophistication, along with the casual stripteases performed by the models in the most unlikely places: behind a column, in the middle of the floor, in an overstuffed chair. That, and the bizarre accumulation of props that littered the three connecting studios: dismantled television sets, bolts of phosphorescent cloth, a motorcycle with sidecar, a row of plaster busts of Roman proconsuls, the bare skeletons of several wall clocks, a collection of stuffed birds, bottles of vermouth covered in colored wax…

"Let's see some ass, sweetheart. This is pantyhose, not grape juice."

"Give me more light here in front."

"Where's the wide angle, Rolando?"

"All right, let's get both of them in there. You, with the tux, here on the left."

Señorita S—Márgara Duran—had a wonderful pair of legs. (Maybe that was the secret: to advertise pantyhose, a pair of legs; to advertise watches, a beautiful wrist; to advertise sanatoriums for consumptives…) She looked tired. Héctor leaned against a wall and waited near a cluster of spotlights on tripods and stacks of boxes full of airline brochures.

"Rolando, I'm exhausted."

"Just one more, darling. Got it."

The woman slouched out of the circle of bright lights and walked toward Héctor.

"Márgara Duran?"

She looked at him curiously. She was only very slightly cross-eyed, and it gave her a certain youthful grace for a woman of around forty.

"I need to talk with you."

"If you can wait a minute, we can go have coffee in the café on the corner."

Héctor nodded. The woman started to take off her pantyhose.

"You look kind of tired yourself. You can wait for me there if you want."

Héctor nodded.

"Go ahead, I'll be there in ten minutes. Just give me a chance to get this makeup off."

The café was empty. Three tables and a lunch counter, a few cakes inside a glass case. A handlettered sign on the wall said they served fresh *horchata*.

Héctor held his head between his hands and returned to his thoughts: the same story as always, another man's life, another man's death. Killing. He felt off balance. You were supposed to have certain reactions to death, violent reactions. Human beings weren't born to go around killing one another. Or were they? The question buried itself between his eyebrows and stayed there.

Did he like it? The power, the taste of power over another man's life. The crucial accuracy in the moment of squeezing the trigger, his cold-bloodedness, quick reflexes, the unexpected advantage of having only one eye to aim with, oddly making him a better shot than he ever was before. Where had he learned to shoot like that?

"I'm sorry if I made you wait long."

Héctor raised his head and looked at the woman.

"What would you like to drink?"

"You've got a bad eye too."

"It's a glass eye."

"Accident?"

Héctor nodded.

"Who killed Zorak?"

The woman gave him a hard stare and her face changed. The youthful self-confidence of a model worn out after a ten-hour shoot gave way to the tense features of a mature woman exhausted by the brutal effects of the last six years of living.

"Are you a reporter?"

"An independent detective."

"What's that?"

"I'm not a cop. I don't buy or sell anything. I work alone. And I need to know because the same people who killed him want to kill me."

"I know they killed him. I don't know who did it, but I do know how. I could never prove anything, though. What for? Nobody cares."

"The newspapers said that his wrist was badly abraded. That shows that it wasn't a problem with the safety hookup. It was the helicopter…"

"I was there. I saw it happen. Captain Freshie talked with the pilot afterward. He said it was an updraft. But if that's all it was, then why did they make such a big deal about the bad hook-up?"

"Who's Captain Freshie?"

"One of my husband's friends, from Durango. After he became famous, Captain Freshie showed up one day asking for work, and Zorak hired him as his bodyguard."

"Why did he need a bodyguard?"

The woman didn't answer.

"What about the old man, Leobardo? And the other one, the guy who owned the nightclub?"

"They were his helpers, his assistants. Leobardo made most of Zorak's props in his shop. They helped him with his act, with the magic tricks and the escape stuff. He used to practice with us for hours and hours."

"Zorak trained the Halcones, didn't he?"

"Who?"

She knew, but she was afraid to say so.

"Who paid off the pilot to do the trick with the helicopter?"

"My husband had enemies."

"Who were his enemies?"

"His competitors, they were jealous of his success. He was number one, and no one could come close to him—"

"That's horseshit and you know it…Zorak was killed so that he wouldn't tell what he knew about the tenth of June. He held a privileged position during the training of the Halcones, and he knew who the commanders were and who was behind it all."

"I don't have the slightest idea what you're talking about."

Héctor stood up.

"You know what, Señorita S? You can pay the bill."

He walked out of the café without looking back.

He cut himself shaving and he stood in front of the mirror watching the thin trickle of blood run down his cheek. It was enough to make him decide to let his beard grow. He was in the middle of the jungle already, and if the vines opened up to let him pass, and the cannibals were on his trail, and the air was full of the smell of death, then the blood might as well run down his face, and he might as well let his beard grow.

Carlos entered the bathroom and bumped into Héctor, interrupting his thoughts. He took his toothbrush from the medicine cabinet and put some water in a glass.

"You've got to find somewhere to stay," he said.

"I was thinking about going to a hotel. A different one every night," said the detective, dabbing at the blood with a piece of toilet paper.

"Not a good idea. Cheap hotels are always full of cops. Secret police, state police, city police…it's like a second home to them."

Héctor threw the bloodied paper into the toilet and pushed the handle. Carlos brushed his teeth.

"What's the best place to get some thinking done in Mexico City?" asked Héctor.

"The Pino Suárez subway station, behind a column, around seven at night, with thousands of people going by," answered Marina, squeezing into the bathroom with them. Héctor leaned back to let her get to the medicine cabinet. She took out her toothbrush.

"The restaurant on the top floor of the Latino Tower," said Carlos.

"The swings in the Parque España," said Héctor.

First they'd gotten him involved in the murder of Zorak's two assistants, without his ever having asked for the part. Then they'd cordially invited him to leave the country. Then, angered by his lack of cooperation, they'd set about hunting him down. And now they wanted to avenge their dead.

If anyone could make any sense out of this mess, it isn't me, thought Héctor, as he swung softly back and forth.

Chapter X

A good detective never marries.
—*Raymond Chandler*

There was nothing in the newspapers. Commander Silva (When would he cease to be just a name?) wasn't talking to the press; Melina was in the hospital; Zorak's three buddies, with their throats slashed by the Chink, lay on slabs in the morgue, along with the Chink himself and three of his own friends, victims of Belascoarán's .45 and El Gallo's Wild West six-shooter. Nothing but peace and tranquility as far as the eye could see…He might as well take a vacation to Acapulco, change jobs, get married…

Suddenly he wasn't joking anymore. If everything around him had gone crazy, like a radio play written by Porfirio Díaz or Cuauhtémoc doing detergent ads on TV; if the bad guys were eternally in power, if everything was going to remain the same, he might as well commit the ultimate madness and get married again.

Anything would be better than to continue this crazy dance through the city, not daring to go home, unable to relax in the old armchair in his office and watch the clouds float by, with no time to feel sadness or nostalgia, and with the weight of three dead men heavy in his blood.

But who could he marry?

The pang of love deferred hit him hard between the eyes. Too much loneliness these last few days, too much for a one-eyed independent detective.

He was eating a huge sundae, with three different kinds of ice cream, bananas, strawberries, whipped cream, and nuts, in an ice-cream parlor in the Colonia Santa María that he hadn't been in since he was a teenager. It was there he decided to get married again.

He realized that he could sense death waiting for him in the midst of this strange story full of Romans and Halcones, and he didn't want to die without having felt, one more time, that dose of daily love. He wanted just one week of married life before leaving Mexico City forever.

He was about to laugh at himself, him and his crazy ideas, when he raised his eyes and saw his reflection in the mirror behind the counter.

It was him all right. The scarred, unmoving left eye, the sad puppy dog look that sometimes crept into his smile. Thirty-three stubborn, hallucinatory years behind him, and what was to come?

He studied the building with the eye of a medieval soldier about to lay siege to an enemy castle. He took off his jacket and dropped it on the ground. But that left his gun exposed, raw power in a leather holster. So he retrieved the jacket and put it back on. It was a four-story building, with balconies full of potted plants, its whitewashed front broken by a vine that wound down from the roof and into a small tree on the sidewalk. A parrot hung in a cage on one of the balconies. The sun reflected off the windows of the ground-floor apartment and into Héctor's face. Without further prelude, the detective jumped up and grabbed one of the tree's lower branches. He hung there briefly, then slowly hooked a leg around the branch. In Mexico City any public spectacle, no matter how insignificant, instantly draws a crowd, and no sooner was he sitting safely on the branch than a pair of middle-school students, dusty neckties askew and carrying worn-out miniature briefcases, took up position at the base of the tree.

"Bet you five pesos he falls and busts his head open,"
said one.

Héctor hocked a gob of spit at the sinister prophet of
doom, who jumped nimbly out of the way.

"Hey, I was only kidding."

A second branch, a foot and a half higher up, put him
within reach of the balcony with the parrot. A servant on her
way home from the bakery and a man carrying a cylinder of
gas on his shoulder joined the audience on the sidewalk.

"Hiya, good-looking," said the parrot.

Héctor put one foot onto the balcony wall and, tearing
his pants leg on a sharp branch, raised both hands over his
head, reaching for a grip on the bottom of the third-floor
balcony. For a second he teetered, off balance, and it looked
as though he might fall. But his right hand found the concrete lip, and then his left hand grabbed hold. With one
foot he searched for a purchase in the climbing vine, and he
slowly raised himself up. His audience, which now included
a very small girl with an even smaller doll under one arm,
applauded his effort.

"Hiya, good-looking," said the parrot again.

"*Adiós*, stupid parrot," answered Héctor.

He held on tightly to the metal grate that fronted the
balcony, and inched himself upward to where he could grab
on to its upper edge.

Then he pulled himself over the top and brushed the dust
off his trousers. Three floors below, the satisfied crowd dis-
persed, and Héctor stepped up to the balcony's glass doors.

Through the glass he could see the living room,
with its immaculate white rug and a single table in the
middle. On one wall there was a giant map of Mexico
City, full of colored pins and with drawings around
the edges.

She came out of the kitchen, wearing a long, full skirt
that reached all the way down to the ground, and nothing

else. She was barefoot, and her breasts danced softly as she walked. She carried a glass of juice in one hand. Héctor tapped on the window with the tips of his fingers, and she dropped the glass and shouted something that never made it to the detective's ears, blocked by the thick pane of glass. The detective pointed at the glass door, locked from inside. She covered her breasts with one arm and let out a laugh. Then she turned around and went back through the doorway she'd just come out of.

Héctor lit a cigarette. The woman with the ponytail came back into the room a couple of minutes later. She wore a white blouse, and carried a fresh glass of juice. Héctor pointed again at the locked door, but she only smiled, and sat down on the white rug in front of him. Héctor followed her lead and sat down on the concrete terrace.

They spent half an hour like that, face-to-face, separated by the glass, unspeaking, smoking, looking straight at each other, or with their gaze lost somewhere in the distance. Maybe because it's necessary to let love rest before it can heat up again inside you, or maybe because these had been difficult times, or maybe because you can't simply sweep a woman away no matter how many walls you climb, the two of them felt a sadness coming over them. She got up and walked over to a record player underneath the map of Mexico City, then came back and sat down in the same spot. She hesitated, then finally got up again and opened one of the windows that let onto the balcony. From where he sat, Héctor could hear the first guitar chords of a song by Cuco Sánchez. He smiled.

The afternoon light was fading, giving way to a soft, clear dusk, transparent but without brightness. Half an hour later, Héctor lit another cigarette. The woman with the ponytail reached behind her and unfastened the top button of her blouse, then the next one. She would have had to have been a contortionist to undo the third button. Next came the buttons on the sleeves. Héctor sat watching her sad, sweet striptease, overcome by a feeling of extreme loneliness. She pulled the blouse off over her head, once again exposing her breasts. The woman with the ponytail smiled.

It was almost dark now. There were no lights on in the apartment and the room and the balcony were sunk in the last feeble light of evening, augmented by the still-dim beams of the streetlights. Héctor took off his jacket, his shoulder holster, and his shirt, and piled them up at his side. Then he took his pants off. He sat back down and his bare buttocks scraped on the cold floor. He found his Delicado filters in the pile of clothes, lit one, and breathed the smoke deep into his lungs.

"Come on in, you miserable one-eyed detective. You'll die of cold," she said, opening the door.

"They won't be satisfied until they see you dead and in your grave," said El Gallo.

They were sitting on a bench in the middle of the Parque Hundido. A few small children ran past them, dressed in red-checked shirts and blue pants. They shouted a strange litany: "Jingle bells, Batman smells, Robin laid an egg…"

"I'd like to know what started all this," said Héctor. "I've got what's called an unhealthy curiosity."

"An unhealthy curiosity?"

"That's what my ex-wife always said when I got interested in something I wasn't supposed to be interested in."

El Gallo took out a short cigar and rolled it around between his fingers.

"The whole thing stinks. They're watching the office like vultures, they're watching your apartment…"

El Gallo lit his cigar. They stood up together and started to walk.

"How about you, Gallo? How're you holding up?"

"I couldn't stop shaking for two days. It was this weird mixture of fear, revulsion, guilt…But then I told myself: What the hell. Yes, I killed a guy. But I had a good reason for doing it. I hid the gun, and that was that, life goes on. And besides, I'm not the one they're after, they don't even know who I am, just another guy who shares your office."

"You know what, I'm getting married," Héctor said all of a sudden.

"What worries me is that I don't really see a way out of this thing for you. This story doesn't have a happy ending," said El Gallo. Héctor smiled as an avalanche of small children rushed past them.

"Who are they? How many are there? Who's their protector?" asked El Gallo.

"They're everywhere. It could be anyone."

"But who are they?"

"Everyone. All of them, everywhere," answered Héctor Belascoarán Shayne, including a good part of the city in a vague sweep of his hand.

"How's it going to end?"

"When they finally catch up with me, I think," said the detective, his voice serious.

"Maybe an experienced independent detective like yourself could get work in Africa, or in…somewhere far away I mean."

"Who knows. I'm sure there'd be work for an engineer, though. That's why I'm not going," said Belascoarán.

They came out of the park onto Insurgentes. It was a sunny morning, the southbound lane was full of cars. They strolled along until they reached a sidewalk ice-cream cart.

"What are you going to do now?"

"I'm going to get married."

"I mean, what else?"

"I'm going to find out as much as I can, and fuck them over as much as I can."

"Yeah, but who's them?"

"The bad guys," said Héctor. He asked the ice cream vendor for a double scoop of chocolate and lemon.

"What the hell kind of combination is that?" said El Gallo Villareal.

It was one thing to have a pleasant stroll with El Gallo through the Parque Hundido and another thing altogether to walk alone through the city with the weight of three dead men on his back. This thing of "the bad guys" wasn't enough. He had to give them names, faces, places, a context. Héctor, who had never exactly thought of himself as a man on a collision course with authority, saw the State as something akin to the witch's castle in *Snow White*, from which emerged not only the Halcones, but other things too, like his own engineering degree, or the crap you saw on television. There were no gray areas there. It was all one big infernal machine that it was best to keep as far away from as possible. Other times he saw it all as a set of characters to be matched up in a series of epic duels. Both ideas appealed to him. In this corner, wearing the black trunks, the challenger, Mikhail Bakunin; in that corner, the State. Or Sherlock Holmes vs. Moriarty. In between the two extremes there was nothing, and maybe that was what lay at the source of his grudge match against the unidentified "bad guys." In them, both of these visions came together.

He changed channels and hit upon a formula that was more manageable, although perhaps less exact. Los Halcones. The tenth of June. Zorak. The subway police, forty of them still operating as a group. Captain Estrella as the visible head.

If there were only just forty, thought Belascoarán. If there were just forty of them, there could be a limit, an end: the three that I killed, the one that El Gallo got, one more tied up naked in the Desierto de los Leones and out of action at least temporarily:

$$40 - 5 = 35$$

Having arrived at this encouraging conclusion, he set out to reconnoiter the streets.

❖ ❖ ❖

Carlos had been drinking. It showed in his puffy lips, his narrow, bloodshot blue eyes. Marina didn't exactly look like the model expectant mother herself, but she did make the effort to get up and put on water for coffee.

"What's up, Héctor?" asked his brother.

"Why don't you go wash your face in cold water and then we'll sit down and tell each other our problems brother-to-brother," said the detective, throwing his jacket over the back of one chair and slumping down into another.

"If he would only talk to somebody!" shouted Marina, as she put the teapot on to boil on the tiny stove.

"How cold does the water have to be?" asked Carlos.

"Freezing."

Carlos left his pack of cigarettes on the table and went into the bathroom. The diminutive size of the apartment gave the things inside it a human dimension. Everything was within reach, and nearly everything could be utilized with just a couple of economical movements. It was crowded, full of things, but not too full. Héctor liked it because it stood out in contrast with the useless abundance in which he himself had lived a few years ago, and with the chaos that surrounded him lately.

Marina placed two coffee cups on the table and put a soft drink out for Héctor. Her belly brushed the back of Héctor's chair.

"What's it going to be, a boy or a girl?" he asked.

"You're the detective," answered Marina.

Carlos emerged from the bathroom drying his face, his thick red hair falling across his eyes. He squeezed by Héctor and scooted the table out to make room to sit in the chair against the wall, then picked up a coffee cup and set it in front of him. Marina sat down and smiled.

Héctor finished off his soda and took out his pack of Delicado filters.

"Smoke?"

Carlos and Marina each took a cigarette.

Héctor breathed the smoke out through his mouth and nose, like he used to do in high school. A photograph of Ricardo Flores Magón stared at him from the wall. Underneath the picture was a quote that he'd previously come to think of in relation to his brother: "The cliff's edge does not scare us, falling water is so much more beautiful."

"So, the government forms the Halcones at the end of 1970 and puts them into action on the tenth of June '71. Then it demobilizes them..."

"There was too much scandal, things were getting out of hand," said Carlos.

"I don't know if you can say they were actually demobilized..." said Marina.

"As a functioning unit..."

"If they never officially existed, then they couldn't exactly be demobilized," pointed out Carlos.

"Whatever you want to call it. But after they're broken up they go on to become part of the subway police, and eight years later, they're still there, at least a big chunk of them, forty or so, under a Captain Estrella—captain of what I don't know. That's one part of the story. The other part is that Zorak dies in a suspicious accident two years after the Halcones are demobilized. Who killed Zorak and what for? The Halcones? The cops? And why has the whole thing come to the surface again eight years later, when it seemed like it had all ended with Zorak's death? First Don Leobardo shows up with his throat cut in the bathroom of my building, then they send me the photograph of Don Agustín. Both of them worked for Zorak."

"Your two little dead men," said Carlos.

"My first two," continued Héctor. "And that was the start of a wild goose chase that finally brings me up against Captain Estrella and his subway goon squad. And the Zorak-Halcones connection. They tell me to keep my nose out of it, but they're the ones who got me into it in the first place…It doesn't make any sense. Then they kill this guy Captain Freshie, the last of Zorak's assistants, and they've been trying to hunt me down ever since. I know who they are, but I don't have the slightest idea what it's all about."

Héctor stood up.

"Got any more soda?"

Marina pointed to the refrigerator. He had to move a broom and a couple of buckets to open the refrigerator door. There were three Cokes and an Orange Crush. He picked the Orange Crush.

"What are you going to do?"

"What can I do? I'm going to keep on pushing."

"How much longer?"

"As long as they let me."

Marina and Carlos exchanged looks. Marina spoke.

"It's crazy, Héctor…Take a good look at it. The government's behind the whole thing. You've got to see the big picture. It would be like if you were trying to gather evidence to show that the president stole a bunch of money. Maybe you could prove it, but you're never going to be able to take it to trial."

"So what the hell am I supposed to do?"

Marina and Carlos were silent. Héctor took a long swallow of soda pop, lit a cigarette and savored the smoke.

"It seems kind of crazy to tell him to go underground. Where would we send him? Today, in the middle of the so-called political opening. Ha ha," Marina said to Carlos. "A scandal this big, the opposition parties wouldn't try to cover it up. Can you imagine what the CP could do with something like this?"

"But suppose you take your analysis a little further," Carlos said, speaking to Marina. "All he's got so far is the connection between the Halcones and subway cops. And evidence that they killed three nobodies who used to work for some crummy magician. Suppose you go public with it. The most you would get out of it would be to force the ex-Halcones out of the subway police. Where does that get you? The really important thing is to find out why they're so eager to erase their connection with Zorak."

Héctor looked from one to the other.

"Suppose you get rid of the forty in the subway. What are you going to do next? Go after the Judiciales? Then what? Are you going to take on the secret police? Then the army? You'd have to be nuts. You're going to get yourself killed."

Héctor nodded. "But I'd like to know why," he said.

"Give me a fucking break, Héctor. Why? Because this is Mexico, that's why," said Marina.

The rest of the afternoon slipped away, full of talk of detective novels, the games they used to play together when they were kids, old grade school teachers. It was as if they had reached a momentary truce with Zorak's killers. Marina reached out her hand from where she sat and opened the door that let out onto the roof, and the sun came in, bathing one corner of the rug with its light. A little while later a cat appeared and stretched out in the light's warm triangle. Around six o'clock, Héctor finished the last Coke. The truce was over.

"Any ideas?"

"First off..." said Marina.

"Because the most..." said Carlos.

"More coffee, Carlangas?" asked Marina. Carlos nodded.

She stood up and walked two steps into the miniature kitchen. She looked funny, with her disproportionately big belly, for someone who used to be so skinny. She looked beautiful. Héctor was surprised to find himself smiling. He watched Carlos admiring Marina. At least whatever was bothering Carlos didn't have anything to do with him and Marina, or with their future child. It was something else that brought the double lines of tension to Carlos's forehead.

"They're keeping them alive, that much is clear," said Marina.

"Who?"

"The Halcones," answered Carlos. "They weren't just dumped there in the subway police as a way to get rid of them forever. Maybe there's more of them waiting in other police units, or in other states. They're alive, and they're planning on using them again."

"That's got to be it. They're holding them in reserve. If they weren't planning on using them again, they wouldn't be making such a big deal out of all of this," said Marina.

"All right, suppose you guys are right. But all the same there's got to be something that's got them running scared right now. Something that would lead them to commit three murders and then come after me. Something connected to Zorak...I'd never seen the three of them before in my life, Leobardo, the guy who owned the cabaret, and Captain Freshie...But the Halcones think that whatever it was that made the three of them a threat, that somehow they passed it on to me. They think that I had something to do with Zorak's three buddies. And whatever that is, it's connected to the Halcones' past, or to something that they're planning, something in the future..."

"Makes sense to me," said Carlos. "More the future than the past. The whole thing with the tenth of June is old news. I don't think the system would have much trouble blowing off warmed-over accusations about something as old as that. How long ago was it that Heberto Castillo raised the whole issue again, and they just forced themselves to swallow a little more shit, and it didn't end up going anywhere. What could Zorak's people have known? I think it's more likely to have something to do with something that's going to happen, something they're planning, the fact that the whole paramilitary group still exists and they're going to revive it for some new operation."

Héctor lit another cigarette and sat thinking in silence. The sun had gone away from the corner of the rug and the cat had followed it. Carlos and Marina held hands across the table cluttered with empty cups and glasses and soda bottles and wrinkled-up cigarette packs.

"By the way, I'm going to get married," said Héctor.

Chapter XI

*If we could get close enough to the tiger,
then we could put eyewash in his eyes to
counteract the effects of the tear gas.*
—Kaliman, from the radio show

They shot at him from less than ten yards away, but the bullets sprayed out on either side of Héctor. One of them knocked a chunk out of the cement wall at his back, another ripped through the lining of his black leather jacket, and another one went through the stomach of a woman walking nearby, shattering her pelvis into half a dozen pieces.

Héctor looked straight into the face of the man who stepped toward him out of the idling car, an M1 rifle at his hip: he was approximately Héctor's age, bug-eyed, his lips pressed tightly together, a lock of dark hair falling casually across his forehead.

The driver's-side door opened and a man in a sport coat got out with a .45 automatic in his hand. Héctor pressed himself against the wall behind him and brought his hand to his gun. But the wall gave way under his weight and he found himself stumbling backward through the patio of a tenement block, backpedaling and half tripping over a tricycle. The echo of the shots still rang inside the closed space, and the wounded woman screamed outside in the street: "*Madre Mía! Madre Mía!*" Héctor gripped his gun in both hands and aimed at the opening made by the metal door through which he'd stumbled, swinging now softly back and forth on its hinges. The man with the M1 ran through the door, and Héctor pulled the trigger at a distance of less than ten feet. The man's face disintegrated as the roar of the shot expanded in the patio air. The second man came in shooting, only to run into the falling body of his now-faceless partner. Two bullets strayed toward a second-floor window, exploding the glass and filling the patio with tiny splinters of light. Héctor fired again, the bullets entering the man's chest and perforating his lung. The man spun around from the impact. Héctor crossed the space between them and put a bullet into the gunman's stomach at point-blank range. The man collapsed to the ground.

Héctor stepped over the body and peered out into the street, thinking clearly that he would never be able to forget that corner of Vertiz and Doctor Navarro, the dirty light at five in the afternoon, the smog, the car, its motor still running, both doors wide open, tires biting into the curb, the woman, moaning now, *Madre mía*. The sound of the shots that wouldn't leave his ears, a pair of taco vendors standing over the wounded woman with the look of men accustomed to violence, accustomed to the oozing puss of everyday existence in Mexico City. He put his gun back into its shoulder holster and walked rapidly in the other direction, crossed the street just in front of a passing bus and lost himself in the Colonia Doctores. His hands shook, and the sound of the shots still rung inside his head, refusing to go away, stubbornly persistent, there to stay, forever. He tried not to think about the face he'd seen disintegrate in front of him under the impact of his bullet.

He was afraid, with a sticky, uncontrollable fear that left its mark plainly on his body. It started as a brutal tug at the corner of the scar over his eye, turned into an irresistible need to urinate, drifted away to become a suffocating pressure on his chest, came and went as a trembling in his hands, an acid putrefaction on the top of his mouth, a nausea in the pit of his stomach. No matter how much they tell you that the fear is all in your head, you know for a fact that it's in your body, in the knowledge of death that you carry inside your own skin. Was everything going to be this way from now on?

❖ ❖ ❖

He watched for half an hour outside the hospital until he had satisfied himself that there was no visible police presence. On the outside, at least—nothing interrupting the regular flow of new mothers with bouquets of flowers, worried relatives, crying women, the occasional ambulance driving up the ramp to the emergency entrance, an athlete with a broken ankle who came out for a brief walk around the garden, a half dozen children playing out front. If there was any special security it would be on the inside, on one particular floor, in one particular room.

With a white smock he'd picked up at El Tranvia Discount Uniform Supply, wearing a cardboard grin worthy of a toothpaste ad, Héctor walked into the hospital as Dr. Belascoarán. He lit a cigarette as he got off the elevator on the third floor, and walked with a doctor's air (a little faster than normal, his gaze lost somewhere in the distance, a standard smile on his lips) toward room 316. Nothing. He put his hand in his pocket, feeling the metal of his gun, and pushed the door open. A man sat to one side of the bed watching TV, his right hand stroking the tip of his mustache. Melina slept in the soft bluish light from the window. The man looked at Dr. Belascoarán as he pushed the door closed behind him with the heel of his shoe. But by the time he reacted it was too late; Héctor had his gun pressed to the center of the man's forehead, where it slowly formed a mark on his skin, "like a third eye," thought Dr. Belascoarán behind the shining toothpaste ad grin. If he couldn't escape his fear, at least he could play with it.

"Good afternoon," said Héctor.

The man gripped the metal arms of his chair. Melina sat up in the bed.

"He's got a gun," she said.

With his gun still pressed against the forehead, Héctor stuck his hand inside the man's jacket and pulled out a revolver.

"I'd like to have a talk with you…alone," he told the showgirl, who was now sitting all the way up in bed with a rather idiotic smile on her face. He gestured for the man to stand up, then made him walk into the bathroom and pushed him down onto the toilet. There were no windows. Héctor smiled.

"Your clothes, pal."

"What do you mean my clothes?"

"Let's go. Strip."

The gunman, submissive now, started to take off his clothes. Héctor took them from him and threw them onto the bed. The man had a long scar across his chest; his naked skin was grayish white.

Héctor stepped out of the bathroom, pushed a chair up against the door, and sat down on it.

"If you make any noise, I'll come in and shut you up," he said to the door.

Melina still wore her idiotic smile, so the detective gave her back his own toothpaste grin.

"How many are there?"

"Two, the other one comes at night…They're cops. Or at least they have police ID."

"They're the same ones as before. The same ones that tried to kill you."

He could see the tension in her face.

"I told them I don't know anything."

"If I hadn't gotten there when I did…After Captain Freshie, you would've been next."

"Thanks," she said.

Héctor couldn't figure out how to get the conversation going. He lit another cigarette.

"I told them I didn't know who you were, I said I didn't see anything. I told them how the two men had come in and that they killed Fernando..."

"Fernando?"

"Everybody called him Captain Freshie...I told them that the men had come and killed him, and that they hit me, and then there was all this shooting, but I said I didn't see anything..."

There was silence.

Héctor rapped on the door behind him with his gun.

"How're you doing in there? Are you going to answer, or do you want me to come in and find out?"

"I'm fine," came the muffled voice of the gray-skinned man with the mustache.

"What do these sons of bitches want?" asked Melina, the stripper from the Fuente de Venus.

"That's what I want to know. You knew Captain Freshie, and Don Agustín the owner of the nightclub, and the Roman."

"What Roman?"

"The guy who dressed up like a Roman for your act at the club."

"Don Leobardo."

"Did you know that all three of them used to work for Zorak?"

"Sure, that's all they ever talked about. Zorak this, and Zorak that, it was their glory days. Captain Freshie was his assistant, his bodyguard, really. Don Leobardo fixed up his props for him, coffins with fake panels, trick handcuffs, all that stuff, and Agustín Salas, the one who owned the Fuente de Venus, was his manager. They talked about it all the time."

"Was there anything different about them lately?"

"They seemed kind of mysterious. They'd all get together in Don Augustín's office and talk for hours, with the door closed."

"Did Captain Freshie tell you anything about what was going on?"

"All he ever said to me was, 'What a dish you are, baby-doll.' He was like a broken record. I broke up with him three times, and he still…"

Héctor smiled.

"Where did he live?"

"On Balbuena."

Héctor wrote the address down on the back of a promotional card for a caterer for children's parties that had somehow found its way into the pocket of his brand-new white doctor's coat.

"How about you? How are you feeling?"

"I'm all right now. Aren't you going to take my pulse?" The showgirl smiled again and sat up a little farther in bed, enough to reveal the beginnings of an ample bust beneath an embroidered purple nightgown.

"It wouldn't be a bad idea. But then this fellow in the bathroom here might start to complain."

"I suppose he would," she said, sinking back down again under the covers and staring at the closed bathroom door.

Héctor crossed to the bed, raised her hand, which lay languidly on top of the sheet, and kissed it. Then he pushed the bed tight up against the chair that held the door shut.

"It's been a pleasure. I hope I can catch your show sometime soon," said Dr. Shayne, and, removing the white coat, he became just plain detective Belascoarán.

✳ ✳ ✳

The men who had unleashed this madness were dead. The women, Melina, Márgara, knew nothing. Only *they* had an explanation. Only *they* could explain what the hell Zorak had to do with the Halcones, and why that connection, severed long ago along with a broken helicopter cable, had risen again from the past. Only they could tell Héctor what he had to do with this whole story. And only they could kill him. Was it some kind of a race? To find the answers before they killed him? It was just a stupid, typical fucked-up case of unhealthy Mexican curiosity, the desire to know, to stick your nose in where it didn't belong. He was afraid. He was scared shitless.

He'd gone into a barber shop so he could sit and think without having to watch his back. Outside, a massive downpour unloaded onto the passing traffic. He convinced the barber that he wanted a trim and not a crew cut, then tried to go back in his mind to the beginning of the whole story.

There were the three stupid conspirators, Zorak's old buddies, who undoubtedly knew their former boss's connection with the Halcones. The motive for their triple murder was hidden somewhere in a sleazy nightclub, a rooftop carpenter's shop, and who knew where else (where did Captain Freshie work?). And then something had made them jump—until the others finally got the jump on them. Héctor came into the picture somewhere in between. Something connected him to them. Let's suppose (supposed Héctor, as he lit a cigarette under the barber's disapproving glare) that the three of them decided to hire a detective to look into something that they'd found out, to dig a little deeper than they could, to get some kind of proof, and they'd decide to hire a detective—me. One of them is designated to contact the detective, but another one goes and tells Zorak's killers (that would be Captain Freshie, the last one to die, the one who ran away during their first, ephemeral encounter in the nightclub). And so they cut the two old guys' throats and threaten Héctor, who they think has already become involved.

That could explain how the whole thing started. But what was it the three men knew?

A new fear awoke inside him. The fear of not knowing, the fear of dying stupid.

Captain Freshie had worked as a pharmaceuticals salesman, and he'd lived in a drafty, run-down second-story apartment that the forces of evil apparently hadn't bothered to keep an eye on. By the time Héctor left the building night had fallen, and he didn't know any more than when he'd gone inside an hour earlier. Unless it helped to know that Captain Freshie's real name was Fernando Durero Martínez, and that he'd earned his nickname back in college when he'd led his freshman engineering class in a counterattack against the ferocious hazing of the upperclassmen. That was in 1965. Héctor hurried his step, looking for the entrance to the subway. Now he had another problem; he had to find some place to sleep. And he became aware of an altogether new sensation, as though a bird were flying just behind him, over his shoulder, a bird like a shadow, like a cloud, a barely perceptible beating of wings that made itself felt in the nerve endings just below the surface of his skin and around his spine. He felt cold. He had a fever and a strange feeling of discomfort all over, and the three chocolate bars that he'd gobbled down in a candy shop at the entrance to the subway didn't make him feel any better.

He could forget about his brother's apartment, or his sister's place, the office, the woman with the ponytail. He wasn't about to lead the bird of death to his own people.

He went down into the Zócalo station and wandered around awhile, looking at the pictures on the walls and the scale models of the old city center. Then he went back up and out again, into the neon night, the street decorated for

Christmas. Everyone's in a hurry, we're all in a hurry, Héctor told himself, and started walking nowhere in particular.

The basic problem for a man trying to evade his pursuers is the gradual displacement of common sense by instinct, an instinct that becomes duller and duller until it's reduced to a clumsy reflex stubbornly pushing him to place one foot after another in an endless movement across the urban landscape. So Héctor was forced to make a double effort, to recoup what he felt slipping away and to get his head back in working order. It wasn't simply a matter of escape; he had to evade the enemy, and he had to evade his own fear as well. In a city of fourteen million people, his would-be assassins—no matter how many there were, no matter how many resources they had at their disposal—could never find him if he wasn't himself. He could become an insurance salesman walking through the Zócalo, for instance, or…

That's when the light went on. Inspiration, the old magic. He had to turn the tables on them, take the hunt into his own hands. If they were going to end up killing him anyway the thing to do was to play hard, stir things up, take the fear back to them and throw it in their faces. Once he'd made the decision, right there, under the lights of the National Palace and the Cathedral, and with the cold, lonely flagstones of the Zócalo as his only witnesses, Héctor Belascoarán Shayne went on the offensive. Now the last thing he cared about was where he would spend the night. He spent it keeping watch, like a knight waiting for his dragon, walking, vigilant, through the solitary side streets, the avenues, past the all-night *taquerías*, the VIP's and Sanborn's, the taxis lined up in front of the big hotels, the menudo stands on Mixcoac where drunks went to cure their hangovers, the red-light district behind San Juan de Letran, the run-down nightclubs of the Colonia Obrera. Walking, keeping watch, ever vigilant, depositing his fatigue and drowsiness in a far corner of his mind, while he schemed and figured and plotted out the coming offensive.

❖ ❖ ❖

They always came and went through the rear office door on Pedro Antonio de los Santos, probably because it was easier to park there. After two days of constant observation, using a pair of Zeiss binoculars bought at a pawnshop for an outrageous price, he'd more or less been able to make out their routines. The majority of the ex-Halcones arrived in the early morning (between 9:30 and 10:30), in groups of two or three, then went out again and didn't report back until six P.M. Commander Sánchez was most likely the gray-haired man in his fifties with the large black car. But it was Captain Estrella who really interested him. Estrella rode in a red Ford Falcon, accompanied constantly by two or three bodyguards, one of whom kept a shotgun, wrapped in a piece of cloth, stowed under the front passenger seat.

The attitude of his subordinates, the second-floor office—into which Héctor could occasionally see through the dirty windows—his carefully guarded movements in the red Ford, all set him apart. He was Héctor's man.

"How's it going, man? See anything?" asked his host.

Over the last two days, Héctor had become a shadow of himself. His chin was covered with stubble, his dirty clothes made a noise like crushed cardboard every time he moved, his butt itched, and a tic shivered once every sixty seconds through his good eye.

"Same as always."

"Must be some real babes."

"Not bad."

He'd had the good fortune to find himself an ideal observation post, with almost no effort. He'd simply gone into one of the buildings on the other side of the avenue and knocked on the first apartment he came to on the third floor overlooking the street. The door was opened by a dirty, bedraggled young man, a semipermanent architecture student at the

National University, who was supported by his family (the family was from Coahuila, and the money they sent was obviously intended to keep him at a distance). This strange character invited him in, and Héctor introduced himself, smiled, and explained that he needed to use the apartment for an important surveillance job. The man asked him how long it would last, Héctor told him at least two days, they exchanged smiles, and that was that.

There was the smell of marijuana everywhere, exuding from the walls; and the repeated offer of grapes (it seemed that the family back in Coahuila had convinced their off-spring that he'd be better off spending his Christmas vacation studying for exams, rather than going home for a visit, and they'd bribed him with a couple of boxes of grapes from the family vineyard). Héctor's host assumed that his surveillance had something to do with a marital dispute, because the only time he showed any interest and took a look through the detective's binoculars (like way cool, man) he'd zoomed in on the ass of a secretary filing folders in the subway office. Mostly, he spent his time getting stoned, playing The Doors' "The End" over and over on the stereo, and studying for his exams, now and then asking Héctor for small amounts of money to cover the most mundane expenses (hey, man, I need ten pesos to buy bread; check it out, man, can you let me have 131 pesos and 86 centavos for my electric bill; hey, man, check it out, it's 11 pesos for your soda pop and 6 more for mine). Héctor was more than happy to help out.

Héctor finished his notes and shut his notebook. There was only one thing missing from his plan: the escape. It was growing dark on the second full day of surveillance and his eyes watered; half from the tension, half from the smog that rose up from the avenue at all hours of day and night.

"Hey, man, I meant to tell you. There's going to be a party here tonight. A big blowout."

"What's the celebration?"

"The end of exams."

"They're over already?"

"No. I just don't feel like taking any more."

"What about the water?"

"No, still no water."

The water had been shut off in the apartment for several weeks, but, by now, Héctor was beyond questions of water or personal hygiene. He'd even finally broken down and tasted a few of the sticky Coahuila grapes. But now he needed to solve the problem of his getaway.

"I wonder if I could get you to invite someone to your party for me?"

"No problem, man, glad to do it. But I could use twenty centavos for the phone call, eighty pesos for booze, and ten for some bread. What do you say, man? That'd be great."

Héctor handed him ninety pesos and twenty centavos. Then he gave him the phone number of the woman with the ponytail and a cryptic message. It wasn't very likely they'd have her phone tapped, but you could never be too careful.

❖ ❖ ❖

At eight in the morning thousands of commuters stormed the entrance to the Juanacatlán subway station, while waves of traffic swept by on the avenue, leaving behind a dirty spume of gray smoke, discarded papers, squash seed husks, dust, and dirt. With his dead eye concealed behind dark glasses, Héctor crossed the street, walked one block north, and waited at the corner. Less than five minutes later, the red Ford Falcon drove by and parked in front of the subway offices. Héctor boarded a bus, looked around quickly at the other passengers, and took out his gun. He pressed it to the driver's temple and said:

"Do me a favor, pal. Give that red car that's parked over there a little push, willya?"

The bus hit it full on. One of the Falcon's doors caved in like a piece of tin. The bus driver had followed Héctor's instructions with apparent enthusiasm, maybe because of the gun at his head, maybe out of the pure pleasure of being able to crash without having to take responsibility.

Héctor jumped out of the bus. The Falcon's back door opened and one of the bodyguards jumped out, shotgun in hand. Héctor fired without aiming, missed, and paid for his mistake by having to throw himself to the ground as the double-barreled charge of shot scattered above him, peppering a sidewalk hotdog stand and killing its owner. He shot twice more, hitting the man with the shotgun once in the leg. Captain Estrella and another of his bodyguards dragged themselves out of the far side of the Falcon. Héctor retreated back into the street. A Renault screeched to a halt at his side and the door flew open. Héctor dove into the back seat as the car peeled away from the curb, and the door swung shut.

"I thought you'd never get here," the detective told the woman with the ponytail.

At this point speed was everything. They went south on Avenida Revolución at over sixty, while Héctor glanced through the back window at the chaos he'd left behind. It would take them at least ten minutes to figure out what had happened. Fortunately there wasn't much southbound traffic. The girl dropped him off at Tacubaya station and smiled. As she was about to drive off, Héctor asked her:

"Do you want to get married?"

She looked at him without answering. Héctor took a subway ticket out of his back pocket and went down into the subterranean abyss. Luck was with him. A northbound train pulled in a few seconds after he got to the platform. In this way he returned to the Juanacatlán station, underground, a bare seven minutes after he'd left it. He went straight up to the station office. The confusion continued outside in the street, and the only people he saw as he climbed the stairs to the second floor were a pair of secretaries who rushed past him in the opposite direction, without a second look. Once there, he went straight to Captain Estrella's office, went inside, took out his gun, pulled a chair up behind the door, and sat down to wait.

Chapter XII

The morning light shone like the light of a great desert.
—*Guillermo Prieto*

But the truth is that death is always
the most current of phenomena.
—*Tomás Meabe*

Héctor pushed hard and Estrella fell forward onto his chair, dragging papers across the desk with him. By the time he recovered, Héctor had closed the door softly and stood pointing his automatic at a target half an inch above Estrella's nose.

"Good morning, Captain."

Estrella half closed his eyes to the point where they were two thin, incandescent slits. He didn't show any surprise; his only motion was to rub his shoulder where he'd hit it on the desk.

"I suppose there's something you want to know. Go ahead, ask me whatever you want. It doesn't matter, you're a dead man any way you look at it."

"That makes two of us, then. Now we can have a nice little chat, dead man to dead man."

Estrella didn't respond. The morning light flooded into the office, like in an enormous desert. Héctor scratched the scar over his dead eye with his left index finger. They stood in silence for a few seconds. He had a tremendous urge to turn around and walk out of the office, go away and never come back.

"Why have you been trying to kill me?"

"Because, unfortunately for you, those idiots got you into this mess."

"You mean Zorak's friends?"

"Don't tell me that this has all been a misunderstanding. Don't tell me that," said Estrella. The tiny, porcine eyes opened slightly, and his mouth made a shape that wanted to be a smile. It occurred to Héctor that he'd made a mistake. He had the man with the answers in front of him, only he didn't know what questions to ask, he didn't know how to get the answers he needed. And as always when he didn't know what to do, he took out a cigarette, lit it, held the smoke in as long as he could, then exhaled softly through his nose.

"Captain Freshie told me that the old guys had hired you and I believed him. No, Estrella, that's not the way things are done," the captain spoke to himself, shaking his head slowly. "Just look at how many of my men you've killed, and all over a stupid misunderstanding. I was beginning to wonder why you weren't aiming higher up."

Héctor started to think that the best thing he could possibly do was pull the trigger and then run out, shooting at all of them, at everything.

"Zorak was a two-bit circus magician, my friend, and his three helpers were three poor imbeciles who found themselves out of a job one day when a cable broke on a helicopter. So they started to think and think and think and dig and dig until they finally thought they'd uncovered a bone. Except that bone belonged to me, and no dog's going to bite me and get away with it. Too bad they had to go and get you mixed up in it. I could have saved myself a lot of time and trouble if I'd just checked things out first…"

Héctor stood up and walked toward Estrella. The captain's face changed slowly and fear showed in his eyes. Héctor hit him hard against the temple with the muzzle of his gun, and a thin line of red appeared on the side of his head.

"You don't talk about people that way, Captain," said the detective.

"Calm down," said Estrella, touching the small wound and looking at the drops of blood on his fingertips.

Héctor hit him again in the same place, and Estrella stifled a cry. Keeping his gun pointed at Estrella, Héctor went over to the window. The traffic rushed by as usual, but in silence; there was no noise of horns and engines and tires on pavement.

The sound of a drawer opening made Héctor turn around. Estrella held a gun in his hand. They both fired at almost the same instant. Héctor's bullet hit Estrella square in the middle of his forehead, while Estrella's bullet grazed Héctor's face and crashed through the window behind him.

Blood covered his good eye. Héctor tried to wipe it away with the back of his hand. He grabbed a chair and broke the window. The noises from the street mixed with the shouts coming now from the outer office. He got out on the ledge and lowered himself down, cutting his left hand on a piece of broken glass. He hung for an instant in midair, then thudded onto the ground ten feet below. He got up, with a dull pain in his leg. Limping, he tried to run toward the sound of a nearby motorcycle, gunned to life by the woman with the ponytail. He couldn't see; the blood covered his good eye. Two gunshots sounded behind him and he felt a bullet send off sparks from the ground to one side. Commuters about to enter the subway station ran terrified for cover. In the shadows, a friendly hand took him by the shoulder, fingers digging into his collarbone, and helped him onto the motorcycle. He held tight to the familiar body and felt himself thrown back as the bike accelerated. For a dozen elongated seconds his spinal column waited for the impact of the bullet that never came. Then he finally let his head fall against the woman's back, staining her white nylon windbreaker with his blood.

She weaved through traffic, going south along Revolución. With the back of his hand Héctor tried again to clean the blood out of his good eye. His hair was matted down around the wound, which stung like a burn, only more. As the motorcycle lost itself in the side streets of Mixcoac, he realized that he was still holding his gun in his hand. He put the gun away and kissed the girl behind the ear.

"Are you okay? You scared me," she shouted.

"I'm fine. I'm all right. I'm just a misunderstanding," Héctor shouted over the noise of the bike.

"You're a what?"

"A fucking misunderstanding."

She had intended to take him home with her, but the detective had a preference for corner drugstores that went back to his childhood, and they ended up in the back of a small pharmacy in the Colonia Santa Fe. Claiming to have been in an accident, Héctor cleaned himself up and covered the superficial wound with gauze and adhesive tape. They left the motorbike chained to a streetlight and walked to a dusty sliver of park of the kind common to working-class neighborhoods: short on water, trees, and city gardeners. Héctor limped.

"You see what's going on here? Suppose now I was to go and find the guy who was flying the helicopter when Zorak got killed. And suppose he just happens to have a job with the new governor of Puebla or Durango or wherever, who it turns out is the guy who put together the Halcones in the first place. And he's going to do whatever he has to keep the story from getting out…Or suppose that Estrella turns out to be the cousin of some big union honcho, and the two of them were reorganizing the Halcones to be his personal security force…Or suppose they've been working secretly for the next president…"

"Or maybe they just had an offer to star in next season's Saturday morning kid's show on Channel 13, and they didn't want anybody to know about their ugly past," she said with a smile.

"Whatever. You see what's going on here? Estrella said that if I had only known to aim higher up…There's always a higher up. It's all the same, they're everywhere. It could be anyone, everyone."

"They're going to kill you," she said.

"That's right."

"Are you going to keep pushing it?"

"I don't know."

They came to a soft drink stand at the end of the park. Héctor drank down an entire grapefruit Titan in one long gulp. The woman with the ponytail looked at him disapprovingly. He was a mess, and he drank those disgustingly sweet sodas all the time. Héctor ignored her and gulped down a second soda, trying unsuccessfully to wet his parched throat, which kept wanting to close up tighter and tighter, suffocating him.

They'd agreed to get married later that same day at the courthouse in Coyoacán. Héctor spent the rest of the morning wandering through nameless streets, tripping over his own feet, letting the accumulated tension slip away, sweating it out through his pores in the form of a sticky, nervous perspiration. He was lost in the clouds, walking on soft cotton, filled with a diffuse pain that spread out from his leg and the wound on the side of his forehead. He didn't have anywhere to go, the whole story was suddenly off limits to him. Shut off from him as much as the whole of the last three years were now, three years in which he'd broken with the dreams of a successful engineer and entered into the dream of a lone and independent detective. Dreams, loneliness, the newly unfamiliar city dominated by the shamelessness of power, choked with the corrupt and spoiled air left behind by this whole chain of events. It was inevitable. Carlos had been right three years ago when he'd warned him that you couldn't just skate along forever on the edges of the system, that you had to acknowledge the way things really were. But hadn't he done that? Hadn't he accepted things for what they really were? Hadn't he chosen sides?

The judge was named Leoncio Barbadillo Suárez, and for five hundred pesos he was willing to bypass the usual red tape and also accept the forged blood tests that Héctor had bought in a nearby store. While he waited for the arrival of the woman with the ponytail, Héctor recruited the witnesses they would need for the ceremony from a busload of tourists who had disembarked outside the courthouse: a bookstore owner from Gijón named Santiago Sueiras and three triplets (singers, apparently) named Fernández.

But, despite all his preparations, she never showed up.

Chapter XIII

*Until we die, maybe some day…from loneliness or anger…
out of tenderness…or some violent love; surely of love.*
—*Alfredo Zitarrosa*

Nothing belonged to us. Nothing at all. The city had become foreign to us. The earth beneath our feet was no longer our own. Neither was the nasty little breeze that turned up our jacket collars at eight o'clock at night when we didn't have anywhere to go, when we had no saint with whom to take refuge. The city was no longer our own, not even its sounds. Unfamiliar sounds in back streets illuminated by storefronts and streetlights every twenty-two yards, interspersed by islands of darkness you still couldn't hide in, exposed to the revealing headlights of passing cars. That night in which nothing was our own, after which nothing would belong to us ever again. This country, our homeland, closed itself to us, reduced to the spoils of petty opportunists, cheats and liars, a cynicism dressed up in words that no one believed anymore, words spoken out of force of habit. The country sent the defeated out into the sewers, into the endless night.

Walking and walking, hoping to win a few hours in this race with fear. Walking without a compass, without ever hoping to arrive, hoping never to arrive.

Our lady of the lightless hours, protect us, lady of the night, watch over us.

Watch over us, because we are not among the worst that is left to this city, and yet we have nothing, we are worth nothing. We aren't of this place, nor do we renounce this place, nor do we know how to go to another place from which to yearn for these abandoned streets, the afternoon sun, banana *licuados*, tacos with salsa verde, the Zócalo on the sixteenth of September, the baseball diamond in Cuauhtémoc Stadium, the Christmas specials on Channel 4, this terrible loneliness that torments us with its stubborn pursuit. And this awful fear that forgives nothing.

❖ ❖ ❖

His steps led him to Bucareli, full of light and traffic, back to his noisy office, the old furniture, the old feelings. Dangerous ground, but familiar.

It was raining hard when he got off the bus on Artículo 123. It shouldn't have been raining in December.

The sound of The Platters singing "Only You" came from the record store on the corner, the magical song of so many teenage parties, the song of middle-class apartment blocks and dirty school playgrounds.

He crossed the street in the rain, jumping puddles, trying to see through the thickening downpour.

"Don Jelónimo, three coffees and a dozen donuts to go."

"Don't call me Jelónimo," said the Chinaman.

Héctor gave him his best smile.

While he waited for them to pour the coffee into Styrofoam cups, two cars pulled up in front of the office building across Artículo 123. With his back to the street, Héctor counted out the money, then picked up the bag of donuts and the three coffee cups covered with napkins (all the same, they were going to fill up with water just crossing the street). He balanced it all like a Chinese acrobat and went out into the rain.

One of the drivers saw him coming at the same moment that Héctor perceived the danger waiting for him in the shadowy black cars soaked with rain. The first shot missed by three feet, shattering the window of the Chinese restaurant and burying itself in the arm of a shoeshine boy who had gone inside to get out of the rain. Héctor threw the coffee and donuts to the ground, grabbed his gun, and ran diagonally across the half-flooded street.

He fired as he ran. His second shot hit one of the Halcones trying to get out of the car without sticking his feet in a sewer grate. His next shot hit another one in the leg. He'd almost reached the cover of the newspaper kiosk on the corner when a shotgun blast caught him mid-torso and lifted his torn, broken body into the air.

He fell facedown in a puddle, near death. His hand groped in the dirty water, trying to grab on to something, trying to stop something, trying to keep something from slipping away. Then he lay motionless. A man approached and kicked him twice in the face. They got back into their cars and drove off.

The rain continued to fall on the shattered body of Héctor Belascoarán Shayne.

To receive a free catalog of other Poisoned Pen Press titles,
please contact us in one of the following ways:

Phone: 1-800-421-3976
Facsimile: 1-480-949-1707
Email: info@poisonedpenpress.com
Website: www.poisonedpenpress.com

Poisoned Pen Press
6962 E. First Ave. Ste 103
Scottsdale, AZ 85251